STEELING HEARTS

A CANDLEWOOD FALLS NOVEL

HOMETOWN SERIES

STACEY WILK

To Lori and Carol,
I admire your strength, perseverance, huge hearts, and sense of humor.
You are my party planning Dream Team.

∼

PRAISE FOR STACEY WILK'S BOOKS

Through the Darkness "Wilk pens a heart gripping story that will leave you breathless." *Jen Talty, USA Today Best-selling Author*

The Essence of Whiskey and Tea: "If you enjoy a good series about family and love, then this novel is sure to soothe your soul." *Booktrib*

Time Won't Erase: "The power of redemption shines in this emotional story about second chances." *Caridad Pineiro, New York Times and USA Today Bestselling Author*

Taking Root: "...multiple layers of entertainment." *InD'Tale Magazine*

Whispering Christmas: "She makes you feel deeply for each character as if you a part of the Candlewood Falls family." *Mint Copy Services*

Defining Chances: The author masterfully weaves together real-life situations, creating a narrative that's both thought-provoking and emotionally resonant. You'll find yourself rooting for Ember and Raf as they navigate their troubled pasts and learn to let go of guilt and anger. *Hidden Gems Reviews*

HAVE WE GOT A STORY FOR YOU!

Dear Readers:

Welcome to Candlewood Falls!

Each Candlewood Falls story stands alone. However, the end of one story doesn't mean the end of your favorite characters. They can show up in any Candlewood Falls book at any time.

Candlewood Falls is a unique world of connected stories by different authors whose characters, business, and events appear in each others' stories.

Think of Candlewood Falls as a literary soap opera.

Be sure to check out the Ready for Another Trip to Candlewood Falls page at the end to discover which other books include your favorite characters.

Happy reading!

Stacey Wilk, K.M Fawcett, & Jen Talty

～

CHAPTER ONE

Most people would die for a house with a brick façade, tons of windows, two stories, plenty of property, and more than one guest cottage in the back. Claudia Jacobs was not most people. The mansion she stood before belonged to her now. And she didn't want it.

Perched on the sidewalk staring up at the old house, the afternoon June sun baked her neck like Italian bread. The mansion leered back, not much happier to see her. Its tongue stuck out in the way of a red front door desperate for a fresh coat of paint. The shutters became droopy eyebrows, and the grass needed a good bikini wax or at least a date with a lawnmower.

Humidity ran its hands over her stockingless legs and slicked her skin until her thighs would rub together when she walked. Her feet swelled in her heels, making her cute pink designer shoes ugly and uncomfortable. Summer in New Jersey wasn't much different than Chicago. Hot. Sticky. And full of mosquitos.

Her heart stuck on Chicago. Chicago was gone. Not

off the map gone. No longer there for her. She wanted to go back, but nothing would be the same. Not her former hotel. Not the Chicago River. Not brick oven pizza. Because she had effectively ripped apart the ties that bind.

With nowhere to go, and poised like a statue, she contemplated if she should go inside or hail a taxi and make a run for it. *Oh, right.* She snapped her fingers. Hard to find a taxi in the middle of country land New Jersey.

"Do you need some help?" A younger man, maybe in his late thirties, with dark hair and gray-blue eyes approached her.

When had late thirties become younger? She stifled a sigh. Right after she crossed the fifty line. That was when forty looked a lot like twenty-five with a few more wrinkles.

"Do I look as if I need help?" Her snarky reaction was instinct. Where she was from, taking help from a stranger could be dangerous. Establishing strength and courage right away was paramount. Gawking tourists were always an easy target.

"You've been standing there for almost ten minutes staring at the house. I thought you might be lost or confused." His simple smile offered no threat nor did his loose body language.

And if he had wanted to mug her, he would've by now if indeed she had been there ten full minutes, oblivious to passing cars and approaching people.

She regarded him closer. Nice-looking. Too whole-some to be a mugger. He oozed boy next door.

"Confused? I haven't lost my marbles if that's what

you're implying." She hoped that day never dawned. She had no one to help her find her keys or shut off the burner if she did.

The sum of her existence included her career, her assistant Talbot and her son Corbin who was like a nephew, and the collection of suitcases beside her. A pretty sorry existence at that. But when she lost her job at The Barry Watson as hotel manager, she found out quickly who her real friends were.

"I'm not implying anything." This young stranger held up his hands in surrender. "My name is Van Wilde. I live next door." He pointed to the house over his shoulder. "Can I give you directions to somewhere?"

"No, thank you. I'm where I need to be." Unfortunately. Or fortunately, she supposed. She could be homeless. At least Aunt Georgette had provided a roof to live under. "This was my late aunt's house."

Aunt Georgette must've lost her mind in her final years. *God, was that in her genetics?* Leaving that old house to Claudia made no sense except that Claudia was Aunt Georgette's only living relative. They rarely spoke and visited less. In fact, she hadn't been here since she was a teenager.

Where had Aunt Georgette been all the years Claudia and her mother had struggled? They could've used a room or two in that oversized home during the difficult times. Georgette was not exactly the warm and fuzzy type and had kept her distance. No one wanted the stain of failure all over their expensive clothes. Now Claudia had the burden of dealing with the house and all its belongings.

"Oh, you're the new owner. It's nice to meet you. I'll

be working on the house, doing the renovations. Whatever they might be."

"You must work for Dean Hunter." The contractor she had called based on Aunt Georgette's lawyer's suggestion.

"I do. Are you sure you don't want some help carrying your suitcases? You seem to have a few." He choked out a laugh.

She had packed almost everything in her closet, unable to part with much. Her belongings translated to three suitcases to check at the airport, one carry-on, and her oversized tote. She had struggled at baggage claim and in the Uber from the airport. She would need her car to get around town, but that was being shipped—a parting gift from her former employer. The shipping. Not the car.

Talbot had traveled ahead of her, leaving her alone without help. Not that she was blaming Talbot who had her own life and concerns. Claudia respected that and gave Talbot the space she needed.

Claudia was not one to treat the people who worked for her as anything except equals. She knew what it felt like to be handled as if she were the dirt on someone's shoes. She had wanted Talbot to come ahead and get settled because now they both were stuck in Candlewood Falls until she sold this house, and they could move on.

Van stared at her with puppylike anticipation. *What was it he had said?* Oh, right. Suitcases.

"No, thank you. I'll manage." She would be soaked through with sweat by the time she had dragged all her bags into the house. But she needed to exert her independence as a reminder to herself that she could still handle whatever came her way.

"Are you sure? You're dressed kind of nice to carry that stuff."

"I've got it. Really. But thank you." Sneakers and a pair of shorts would be better than her heels and her white tulle skirt, but she hadn't had time to change before the flight. She would wear a more suitable outfit if she knew which bag she had packed with those clothes. No point in wasting precious time looking. The skirt and the heels would have to do. Her back might hate her later, but a few stretches should work out the kinks.

She preferred to dress up for most occasions anyway. The armor of nice clothes and great hair told everyone that she was someone to be taken seriously.

"Okay, then. If you need anything, don't hesitate to knock on my door."

"Thanks." She forced a smile because knocking on his door or anyone else's would be the very last thing on her list. She had no interest in making friends. No one made new friends at her age. She needed to stop saying *at her age.* Fifty-four was hardly old. Just older than before and older than this guy.

Van offered a small wave and disappeared behind the bushes. She lost sight of him as he rounded the corner of the large arborvitaes at what must be the property's edge. She should ask for a copy of the survey. She didn't want her new neighbor arguing about block and lot sizes.

She looped her bag onto her shoulder and heaved the biggest suitcase against her thigh. The faux leather crinkled her skirt and banged her knee. Maybe the help would have been beneficial.

Letting herself into the house with a vintage door key, she dropped the bags in the large foyer with a split staircase. The key was pretty with its cuts and patterns, sitting heavy on her hand. An antique that any collector would love to use as a decoration. A modern key with a security camera and a direct line to an alarm company might be better. She had to remember. She wasn't in Chicago any longer. People in Candlewood Falls probably didn't even know what locks were.

After three trips, the luggage congregated in the house like a tour group waiting for their next stop. Sweat ran down her back and pooled under her bra. She had abandoned the heels after trip two and now her feet were dirty.

At some point, she would claim a bedroom and lug all her stuff up there, but for now, she would hope the water worked and pour herself a cold glass.

Before she could take a step to quench her thirst, her phone rang out an Elton John song from deep within her purse. Someone was calling. Carter River's name flashed on the screen. Aunt Georgette's lawyer. What could he want? She thought they were mostly settled, except she hadn't signed any final papers. In her rush to pack up her old life and start anew, she had missed that detail.

"Claudia Jacobs." She searched for the kitchen, bumping into it at the back of the house. She stifled a gasp at the beautiful floor-to-ceiling windows, letting the professionally manicured lawn and gardens in like well-dressed guests at a party.

"Hello, Claudia. It's Carter River. Do you have a minute?" His voice was raspy with age.

She had a lot more than a minute. "I have a quick second, sure."

"Wonderful. There's a few more things we need to go over about your aunt's estate. We can do it on the phone or you can come in to the office."

"Go ahead and give it to me straight." She had no desire to shove her feet back into those heels at the moment and find her way to his office. Whatever it is that he had to say, he could say on the phone or email it over to her. What she really needed from this guy was the name of a good real estate agent.

"Your aunt put stipulations on the will."

"What kind of stipulations? And why am I just hearing about them now?" If Aunt Georgette had some kind of condition for her to keep ownership, Carter River should've made that clear up front. Hopefully, the mortgage wasn't saddled with a lien.

"Georgette had strict instructions not to mention any of her conditions until you arrived at the house."

"How did you know I was here? Never mind. Small-town stuff, right?" She had no idea how many cars or people had passed her while she outstared the house. But someone had realized the stranger was in town and couldn't wait to get on the party line to spread the word.

"Afraid so. My assistant saw you on the sidewalk. You know, now that I think about it, it might be better if you came in to discuss this. It would be easier in person. I have time now if that works."

"Let me ask you one question first."

"Go ahead."

"Can I sell this house?" She had no intention of staying in Candlewood Falls with its little shops on Main

Street. Each one more adorable and welcoming than the last. Where little old men swept sidewalks outside their stores, waving to kids on bicycles. Or where women met at a knitting club above a yarn shop. Not that she knew if a yarn shop existed in this town, but if she were a betting woman...

Real life was hard and unfair with many disappointments that skinned knees and broke hearts. She belonged in Chicago with its gritty streets and straight-lined skyscrapers and harsh winters. Not Candlewood Falls, soft, warm and welcoming, like a grandma with fresh fruit and iced tea.

"We can talk about your options when you come in. Can you be here in ten minutes?"

Didn't sound as if she had a lot of options. "I'll need to call an Uber."

"Oh, that won't be necessary. You can walk from the house. If you were further in town, then yes, you'd need a car. If you don't have one, you'll want to get one. I can give you the name of a reputable guy."

"I'll let you know." If she could be out of here in a few short weeks, maybe she could do without a car.

"That's fine. Grab a pen. I'll give you a couple of landmarks near the office."

"That's okay. If I can make my way around Chicago, I'm sure I can travel a couple of blocks to you. I'll see you soon. Goodbye." She hit the end button before he could explain the way. There couldn't be too many turns. She'd pop it in her phone.

She found some old juice glasses in the cabinet. The water poured from the spout with enough pressure to bring a sigh of relief to her lips. Too bad she didn't have time for a quick shower. Not before she unpacked some of her things and she didn't want to make Carter River wait.

Patting under her arms and her boobs with a napkin, she shoved her aching feet into her cute pink heels and headed out.

She would sell this house. And nothing and no one, not even Aunt Georgette from the grave, would stop her.

CHAPTER TWO

S ilas Wilde needed to sit before he fell on his ass. He leaned against the hot bumper of his pickup instead. A silver maple had crushed his house. The large tree had to be eighty feet tall and had lain across his roof—what was left of his roof—sunbathing.

Today's clear blue sky showed no signs of yesterday's storm. Hard to believe the weather had grabbed that maple between its hands and ripped her right out of the ground, delivering her to Silas' cabin. He hadn't been home when the storm struck—lucky by all accounts.

He had been at his daughter's, getting some quality time with the new baby. Hadley Ransom had made him a grandfather again and that little girl with her bald head and chubby fists had stolen his heart from the second she laid her dark eyes on him. She had saved his life, literally. He might not have heard the cracking of the roots over the high winds if he had been home.

His cabin was a small house with two rooms and a loft. Some would say not a house at all, but it was his and where he had lived for the better party of thirty years. He enjoyed his isolation in ways others didn't understand. And he didn't care to explain.

"You can always stay with us," his son Brad said, standing beside him with his muscular arms crossed over his broad chest. Brad was as much a friend and coworker now that he was almost forty as he was Silas' son.

He glanced at Brad and the pride that never seemed to stop surprising him washed over his skin. He could not ask for better children than Bradford and Brooklyn.

"Thanks, son, but I don't think so. Too many people in your house." He loved each and every one of them. He did. Oh, hell, his other granddaughter, Brad's daughter, Winter lit up his life like the hot summer sun at noon. Being a grandfather had some amazing perks he had learned, and he was secretly glad he was still young enough to enjoy those grandkids. He might have a few extra aches and pains at fifty-nine, but he could keep up with the best of them.

He loved Brad's fiancée Lyra too. Even her two boys who were full-on teenagers now. He was lucky to have so many people in his life to love and who loved him back. But he was used to his solitude and at his age, he wasn't about to change his ways. He had lived off the grid since his kids were not much older than Winter was now at eleven.

"Dad, it's temporary. You can't stay here." Brad pointed to the house as if he couldn't see for himself he was in trouble.

"I'll figure it out." He could pitch a tent at the

orchard. His father's place was on the family's property. He could use the old man's bathroom, if needed.

"I guess you could move in with Uncle Huck for the time being." Brad pulled out his phone and took photos of the damage. Not a bad idea, and since he didn't have a fancy phone like that, he couldn't very well do it himself.

"Can't. Petra's house isn't done yet. She's living at Huck's with Mav and Paige. Huck is in his glory, not that he'd ever say those words out loud." His older brother, Huck, had become a changed man over the past year or so. If Silas hadn't watched it with his own eyes, he would never have believed it.

Brad turned, holding the phone in midair. "You're kidding? He likes having them all there? He's been complaining about it for months."

"You know Huck." Silas was the fourth of five Wilde brothers with Huck directly ahead of him. He was closest to Huck even with Huck's ornery personality and sometimes skeptical life choices. But his older brother had mellowed since his wife passed. People could always change.

"I know Huck as well as anyone. He makes my guys in the fields nuts almost every day. What about Brooklyn's place? They have extra rooms in that old farmhouse." Brad went back to taking photos.

They circled the side of the cabin. From there it almost looked as if the roof was made of leaves. "Brooklyn is up all night with Hadley. I'd just be in the way. And Cordy is in town to help her and Caleb with the baby for a month or two." Cordy was an unconventional grandmother, but she and Silas always got along. Especially during the years Silas had to raise his kids alone. Cordy had jumped in and helped, exasperated by her daughter's absentee behavior. Made all the sense in the world that Cordy would visit Brooklyn and help her out too.

"You like Cordy."

"Everyone likes Cordy. Doesn't mean I want to live with her or her with me. I can stay at Georgette's place for now. At least until the tree is removed." He hadn't thought about Georgette's place until now. It was empty since her recent passing. No one would bother him there. It might be close to town, closer than he liked, but getting his cabin back into shape couldn't take all that long. He didn't need much.

"You're going to stay in that huge house that needs the black mold removed?" Brad arched a brow.

They walked around back for the last of the photos and retraced their steps to the trucks. They couldn't make a complete circle because the trunk of the maple with two feet of dirt around its roots was in their way.

"I'll stay in the guesthouse. It's in decent shape. Better than the stone cottage Georgette used for storage for fifty years." The guest cottage had a living space, one bedroom, and a full kitchen. He hadn't owned a full kitchen in his house since he moved into the cabin. They had made do with a wood burning stove and as he got older, he added a hot plate for quick fixes.

"Do you know who Georgette left the house to? Is there any chance this person wouldn't want you there?"

Georgette hadn't any family that he knew of. She had been his mother's best friend and after Mom had died, he had kept an eye on Georgette over the years. He had even taken to tending to her garden because she fired so many people no one would work for her anymore. He had known what she liked and did it without a lot of talk between them. Something they both appreciated.

"She might have willed it to the town. Better if it was the historical society. They'll fix it up and make it a museum or an office building of some kind. Carter will tell me when I have to be out. If the cabin isn't finished by the time the new owners take over, I'll sleep at the orchard under the stars."

"I know you're still pretty young, but aren't you a little old to be roughing it that much?" Brad punched him in the shoulder.

"No better place for me than outside with my trees. But I know how you and Brooklyn worry, so I'll stay at Georgette's for the time being. Good enough?"

He had his children when he was so young he could barely drink legally. He had married and divorced their mother so fast his head had spun. He thought he had found the woman for him, but all he had found was a lady who wanted things that shined like gold and cost as much. She had thought she'd married the prince of an empire when all she had married was a farmer.

"Well, I'd prefer you stay at Georgette's than camp out at the orchard. No one would be there if something went wrong."

When his ex-wife had discovered her mistake, she had run so fast from Candlewood Falls her feet hadn't touched the ground. And she had forgotten to take her children with her. Not that he minded. He preferred they stayed with him and his ex had made that easy.

"No one lives with me here either." He appreciated

the concern, but he had no plans to allow his children to take care of him. Ever. He would take care of himself.

"Kind of my point. Do you need help bringing anything to Georgette's?"

"Nothing to bring. I need to pick up a few things though." He would stop in town and get the essentials. Probably some groceries too. He could take advantage of that kitchen. Not 'cause he missed having one, oh no. Just because it was there and it was better to keep the appliances in use for the new owner.

"Will you at least come to our house for dinner?"

"Can't say no to that." The kitchen could wait until tomorrow to be used. He wanted to have his family around him right now. Seeing a big old tree lying across his house put his mortality into check again.

Brad's phone rang. With a shrug, he answered. "This is Brad."

He watched while Brad listened, then handed the phone to him. "It's Carter River for you."

He had a cell phone because Brad and Brooklyn had bought him one, wanting to be able to reach him and make sure he was okay. But he rarely carried it or kept it charged, angering his kids. He'd lived in this town his whole life. His family had been here growing apples for generations. All anyone in town had to do was holler *Silas* and someone would hear it and relay the message.

He took the phone. "Hello?"

"Silas, you are impossible to get a hold of. Man, you need to get yourself a cell phone already."

"I have one." Well, he had one. It was in his house under branches and leaves.

"Never mind that. Can you come into my office? I need to talk to you about something."

"I've got a bit of a problem on my hands out at the cabin. Can this wait?" He would have to make some calls to get the tree removed. Then figure out the full damage and start the rebuild. He would need help this time. He wasn't in his twenties anymore. Building another cabin alone would take too long, and he didn't want to live at Georgette's longer than he had to.

"It's important. It can't wait," Carter said.

"Something wrong? You sick?"

"Not sick. Work stuff. Come to my office right away. I'm waiting." Carter ended the call.

He handed the phone back to Brad. Carter wasn't one for exaggeration. He couldn't imagine what Carter had to talk to him about, but it wasn't the ordinary where should they play poker this time type of thing.

"Everything okay?" Brad shoved the phone in his pocket.

"I don't know. Said it was important, and he wanted to talk. Work stuff. He wouldn't take no for an answer. Guess I'll be meeting him." His curiosity was piqued. He loved a good mystery. As long as he didn't have to be involved.

"Are we being sued?"

"I don't know. Won't be the first time. But I don't think that's it." Carter would've said it had to do with the orchard, or he would've just shown up at the orchard, bought an apple cider donut, and talked shop around the sugar coating his mouth.

"I'm coming with you. What time? I'll call over to the

orchard and let them know I won't be back the rest of the day." Brad pulled his phone back out.

"Slow down now. I'll take care of it. Whatever it is. And then I'll tell you all about it at dinner."

"I should be there too, Dad, if it's about the orchard."

"We don't know it's about the orchard." He hoped it wasn't. A problem at the orchard on top of his house problems would be more than he wanted to deal with.

"We don't know that it isn't," Brad said.

"If you start getting excited over nothing, then Huck will want to come with us to the meeting and Sam will get all flustered and start flapping his wings. And Lacey will wring her hands. We'll have to patch Cooper in. Let me see what it's all about first. Then we can tell the others, if necessary. Okay? Can you keep it quiet for a few hours?" Owning a family business was no easy thing. Couldn't make a decision on which way to swing a door without consulting all the owners. And everyone had an opinion.

Brad regarded him for a moment. His son's wheels were turning. Smoke practically came shooting out of his ears tucked under that hair of his. Silas would wait. He could wait out Brad until his son saw some reason.

"Yeah. Sure. I can wait to say anything until I hear from you. I'm going back to work."

"See you, son." He held out his hand. Maybe some fathers would hug their son at a time like this when that son was a full-grown man making him so proud he couldn't breathe. And maybe he should too, but a shake could also say things he found hard to express.

Brad was the kind of son he had hoped for. Strong. Smart. Loyal. Loved the orchard as much as he did and liked being as dirty. They shared so much in common. He was one lucky guy to have lived his life the way he had.

He had wanted for nothing. And had needed less. Only sometimes late at night he longed for the arms of a good woman to wake with. He hadn't found one was all. Women had passed through his life in all shapes and forms, but no one had stuck it out with him. Everyone had turned and run when they saw how he lived. He was better off alone. Just like he told Brad.

Brad shook his hand, said his goodbyes, and slid into his truck, turning it around on the dirt and gravel lane that acted like Silas' driveway. He waited until his son was gone before hopping into his own truck and heading for town.

He would go into town and meet Carter. After that, he would pick up a few things he'd need back at Georgette's and settle in at the guest cottage before heading to Brad's for dinner. He could whip up his chili to bring with him. He only ever made the chili when he was at Huck's house. A full-size kitchen had its advantages. He was willing to admit that much.

Living in town wasn't for him, though. He didn't like being tracked by his habits or being prisoner to the modern conveniences people relied on. He had lived with his well and his outhouse for so long, he didn't know any other way and wasn't so sure he wanted a different way. That's why visiting once in a while was okay, but he always wanted an escape route back to his simple life.

He could be a part of what others said was regular life as long as he could come back here to his cabin and live in peace and quiet with the wilderness in his backyard. That same wilderness had stuck it to him by dumping that maple on his home. Nature. Couldn't trust her.

He stared up at the treetops. "Were you tired of me as a roommate? Too bad. There's room enough for both of us, and I don't bother you none. Your blustering storm won't keep me from living out here with you."

Nothing could keep him from living on his property in the woods.

Nothing.

CHAPTER THREE

Claudia checked over her shoulder to make sure a camera crew wasn't following her, and she had somehow stepped onto the set of *The Andy Griffith Show*. Candlewood Falls was a place right out of nostalgic America.

She had arrived at Carter River's office to find a note for her stuck to the door that said he waited for her at the coffeehouse. *Coffeehouse?* Who changed the location of an important meeting to a coffeehouse? This man must have some kind of caffeine addiction.

Not to mention, but she would, the main tree-lined street of the town was filled with adorable shops on both sides just like she had figured. She passed an antique store, a music store, a florist, and it appeared a new karate studio was going in. Not her kind of exercise. She preferred power walks and weights because muscle mass was important as one climbed the ladder of age.

She came to the corner and the Green Bean with its awning, inviting her inside. Small tables for two lined the sidewalk of the side street. Most of them were full of people in deep conversation. Didn't anyone work in this town?

Yanking open the door, she was met with the deep aroma of a high-quality coffee bean recently ground. She took a deep inhale. The checkered floor was clean and most of the tables in here were also occupied. At the counter was a glass case that offered goodies to go along with the coffee options listed on the menu suspended behind the baristas.

Carter River waved to her from a spot in the corner by the window. He was a handsome man with a receding hairline and trim figure. He adjusted his tie as he took his seat again. She weaved her way over.

"Thanks for coming." He indicated she should sit. "Can I get you a coffee?"

A file was closed on the table and a black pen rested on its cover. A to-go cup with a coffee stain on the lid sat beside him. He folded his long fingers together and appeared as comfortable working here as he might be in his office. It wasn't as if she hadn't conducted business herself in places other than an office, but a lawyer? And the note? Very Mayberry.

"Do they have iced tea here? I would love one of those." The walk over had wilted her all over again. Her face probably had a shiny, freshly polished look about it. She rummaged in her purse for a clip and twisted her hair into a half-hearted French twist.

"They do. I'll put in an order." He slid from the chair and went to the counter.

She would've done it herself, but Carter was quick on his feet. With her back to the window, she soaked in the atmosphere. The place was cute with its chalkboard filled with drink specials. The baristas were all young with big smiles, greeting everyone as they walked up. Much like any coffee shop, people sat with their ears plugged and their faces in a screen. It was actually nice not to have anyone looking for her at the moment. Her busy life at The Barry Watson had kept her going all hours. She was always catering to someone's needs.

Carter slipped back into his chair. "It will be up in a minute."

"Thank you. So, why the change of venue?" She scooted the chair closer to the table.

"Someone is meeting us, and he prefers a more casual atmosphere."

"I don't understand. Why is someone meeting us?" She knew of no one else involved in Aunt Georgette's estate. Unless Carter had already secured a buyer. That would be lovely, but she would need at least a month to get back up on her feet.

"He's part of the stipulations I mentioned. Oh, wonderful. He's here now." Carter stood again and waved. "Silas, over here."

She turned to see who Carter waved at. A tall man with broad shoulders and salt-and-pepper hair walked toward them as if he had all the time in the world. His pepper-colored goatee was a dusting on his chin and dashed with plenty of salt. His lips twitched up in a short smile, revealing laugh lines around his bright-blue eyes, but the lines disappeared as quickly as they came. He might laugh, but it didn't seem to linger, like a flash of lightning, bright, brilliant but disappeared quickly.

His denim button-down shirt was rolled at the

sleeves and left untucked. But not to cover the paunchy belly plagued by older men. He was fit and sun-kissed. Rugged as the mountains. Her toes curled in her pink high heels. Candlewood Falls was full of surprises.

"Silas, thanks for coming." Carter adjusted his tie again. Not that it needed adjusting. "I'd like you to meet Claudia Jacobs. She's Georgette's niece. Claudia, this is Silas Wilde, a good friend of Georgette's."

Silas' gaze raked over her, pausing at her pink heels and then returning to her face. He nodded without expression and pulled out a chair, lowering his long frame, and stretching out his legs. A delicious cedar scent rolled off him.

"It's nice to meet you," she said, extending her hand.

He nodded again but left her hand hanging. "You too." He turned his gaze to Carter. "What's this all about, Carter?"

Clasping her hands in her lap, she tried to ignore the very handsome, but cold man. She bit back a comment about being rude. Besides, she needed to learn her lesson. Her mouth was the very thing that had put her backside in the unemployment sling.

A cacophony of coffeehouse noises echoed around them as the three of them sat there without talking. A barista brought over her drink while a Melissa Ethridge song blasted through the speakers. She wished Carter would get to the point so she could go back to the house and unpack. She had eyed a pool earlier that would do the trick to cool her off.

Carter fiddled with the folder but didn't bring out any papers. His gaze bounced between her and Silas.

"Are you going to tell us why we're here or make us

guess?" Silas said, swiping her straw and tapping it on the table.

She pulled it out of his hand. "I need that, thank you." Plopping the straw through the lid, she allowed herself a large sip.

Silas arched a brow. *Had she slurped?* Or was he not used to people pointing out his inconsiderate behavior. Well, too bad. She was uncomfortably warm after her walk over, and her unreliable hormones decided to act up.

"Let me thank you both for coming. I waited to explain the whole situation surrounding the estate until we were all together. Claudia, I informed you that Georgette left her home to you, but there's more."

The word *more* gave her the tingles. Aunt Georgette might have come through for her after all. She forced her attention to remain on Carter, not wanting to miss a thing he said, but her treacherous gaze did slide over the handsome but ornery man beside her. The front of his hair had a small flip to it. Pretty good hairline for guy who had to be on the plus side of fifty. God, she hoped he didn't use plugs or something worse like a weave.

Carter cleared his throat. "Silas, Georgette left half the house to you too."

"Come again?" Silas leaned forward in his chair.

"What?" She threw her hands in the air, nearly knocking over her iced tea. Now she had to share the income from the house with this guy too? Her aunt never liked her and would make her pay for it from the grave.

"It's a fifty-fifty split. But there are rules surrounding how and when the estate can be dissolved." Carter opened the folder.

"I don't want her house," Silas said.

She said a silent prayer of thanks for that. She was about to object to this arrangement, but Silas had made that easier for her, and he didn't even know it.

"Georgette suspected you would say that, considering your current living situation. If you refuse your share and the stipulations I have yet to reveal, then the house will remain in trust as such time you get your head out of your ass. Those were Georgette's words. She made me promise I would say them exactly. You know Georgette."

A chuckle slipped from her disloyal lips. Between her gaze and her lips, her whole face was against her.

Silas shot her a death glare. She raised her hands in surrender.

Aunt Georgette hadn't changed a wink. When Claudia came to visit as a teenager, her aunt would always embarrass Claudia with her directness. Georgette didn't care who she pointed the hurtful truth at. When she had something to say, she said it. The other person had better be ready.

"Let's hear the stipulations," Silas said, sitting back in his chair again.

"Wonderful. Claudia, in addition to fifty percent of the mansion's worth, Georgette left you a lump sum inheritance."

Georgette had left the pot of gold after all. She tried not to jump right out of the chair with glee. She could sell her half of the house to the good-looking grizzly guy and be out of Candlewood Falls in a few weeks' time. Best-case scenario.

"That's fantastic. When can I get it?" She gripped the sides of the chair to keep from rubbing her hands together as if she were some gambler thinking she held the best hand.

Silas shot her another death glare.

"What?" she said.

"The woman is barely in the ground, and you're ready to stick your hands in the till. Show some respect."

"Who do you think you're talking to?" Maybe she hadn't hid her enthusiasm very well, but this man had no right to speak to her that way. She grabbed her iced tea to keep her hands busy and allowed herself one big slurp.

"I'm talking to a stranger in my town who never paid any attention to a nice lady who was alone most of her life." He held her gaze with his icy one. The blue irises reminded her of a frozen lake at sunrise. Something she would not ever be on because she couldn't skate, but might want to try now.

"Your town? Do you own it? Are you the mayor?" She would not explain to him how her aunt was uncaring to her or her mother. When they were down on their luck, where had Aunt Georgette been? She had never offered a hand up or a place to stay. She had let the two of them live in cars and crappy motel rooms.

He ignored her retort and turned back to Carter. Her blood boiled, but she forced her breathing to slow. Now was not the time to make a scene. She was inches from her goals.

"Go on, Carter. What else does Sticks here have to do to get her money?" Silas hitched a thumb in her direction.

"Sticks? What are you talking about?"

"Those shoes you're wearing. You might as well be

wearing sticks." He pointed at her pink high heels. They did have a skinnier heel, making them fun and flirty. Not that he would know anything about fashion in his faded jeans and scuffed-up work boots.

Wearing heels made her a normal height. When she was flat-footed, she was always the shortest person in the room and people had often referred to her as cute. Kind of hard to be taken seriously at work when the men in the room could look over her head without any effort.

"My name is Claudia. Not Sticks." She tried to regain some control of this conversation.

"I think Sticks fits you." He turned away from her. "Carter?"

Her chest tightened. Every nerve ending in her body wanted her to either get up and march out of this adorable coffeehouse or give this guy what he was good for. But she fought the urge and took another deep breath before her heart leaped through her ribs.

Carter cleared his throat again. "Claudia, you must renovate parts of the house in order to get the house and the sizeable lump sum. You can't sell your half of the house to Silas. In addition, you must empty and decorate the stone cottage by yourself. I've been assigned the task of checking to make sure you don't hire out the work."

Her mind caught on the word sizeable. She needed the money, a sad truth she could try to deny, but wouldn't bother. At least not to herself. She didn't have a place to stay for the time being as her apartment was taken from her when she lost her job. Staying in the mansion wouldn't be the worst.

If she could speed up the renovations, cut a few corners, she might be out in a few weeks. Clearing out a cottage she knew nothing about concerned her. She wasn't used to getting dirty and who knew what she might find. But if she rented a dumpster, she could throw everything away regardless.

"Oh, there's one more thing," Carter said, dragging her from her thoughts.

"What's that?" she said.

"You have to have the stone cottage completed by the garden party." Carter took a sip from his coffee and puckered his lips with a shake of his head.

"What garden party?" She hoped she wasn't going to be required to plan such a party. Not with having to oversee renovations too. A quick online order would provide a few cheap furnishings to throw in place. Nothing to that task.

Silas smirked. "Your aunt hosted a garden party every summer as a fundraiser for a women's shelter. Didn't she ever tell you about that?"

She hadn't spoken to Georgette in years. After Claudia's mother died, she didn't see the point. Georgette never cared about her and hadn't once reached out to see how she was doing or even send a birthday card. How ironic that Georgette would raise money for women who needed shelter when her niece and grandniece had also needed a safe place to live—which Georgette had not provided.

"Of course, she mentioned it. I forgot for a second. When is the party?" She avoided the intense blue gaze of her co-owner and looked at Carter.

"Three weeks," Carter said.

"Plenty of time." She had no idea if that was plenty of time because she didn't know what she was up against with this stone cottage waiting for her. "How long do I have for the renovations?" Those could take much longer if they ran into a problem, but if she really planned out the details, maybe a month.

"Three weeks. Same as the party. And Georgette left money for that. I'm her executor and will take care of the bills. You just oversee the work and make the decisions."

"Renovations in three weeks? Fine." It sounded crazy but she'd be out of this town in a month's time. She'd find a way to make it work.

"Silas, you're planning the garden party," Carter said.

"That's not funny," Silas said.

"It isn't a joke. Georgette wants you to plan the garden party. All of it. If you don't get the party off on time, then you forfeit your share of the mansion. Claudia will own the whole thing."

"And what happens if she bungles the renovations?" Silas nodded in her direction.

"If you can't complete the renovations and have the cottage cleared by the three weeks, Claudia, then Silas will be the sole owner of the house and you don't get the money."

"So, I don't get extra any money if I win, but she does," Silas said.

Carter flipped through the papers in the folder. "Georgette's exact words were, 'Silas Wilde needs money like an apple needs a worm. That's an analogy even he should understand. But he does need to live somewhere other than that godforsaken cabin all by himself.' End quote."

So this man who oozed rugged like sap from a maple tree, also had financial security and apparently some strange living arrangement. She learned a lot from this little, but bizarre, conversation today.

"Can't he and I just sell the house, skip the party, and go our separate ways?" She forced her gaze to Silas'. "Assuming you don't want to organize a flower party or own this house either."

It all seemed simple enough. He had said right off the bat he didn't want the house. Neither did she. She only wanted the money the sale of the house would provide. If all she had to do was clean out a small cottage, that was a manageable task. They could forget about the rest.

Silas turned to face her. His hands were large and rough-looking as if he did work outside. All he needed was a cowboy hat and a horse and he would be right out of a modern day western.

"Who would you want to sell that house to?" he said in his deep, gravelly voice.

She needed to stop noticing this man before she started drooling all over him. In her line of work, she dealt with men in power suits and ties and who wore shoes upward of five hundred dollars. But she always loved the man in a soft flannel and a pair of jeans. She kept that little piece of information to herself, never wanting to reveal that Claudia Jacobs, hotel manager, would rough it. The whole idea had not worked with her image.

"I haven't thought it all out, but most likely a hotel chain. That place is too big for a family in today's market, who want experiences more than objects. It makes most sense for a corporation to own it and take care of it.

Maybe even knock it down and put up a lower-cost hotel for tourists. Some kind of extended-stay."

His eyebrows shot up his forehead. "You think the best thing for that mansion and this town is for a hotel chain to come in and put their ugly corporate fingerprints all over it? You would think that."

"How do you know what I would think?" Her iced tea was empty. She shook the ice cubes at the bottom of the cup, but only air came up through the straw.

He arched that damn brow again and turned back to Carter. "I'll plan the party in three weeks. If I succeed, I own the house, right?"

"That's correct," Carter said.

"Fine. How hard can planning a party be?" he said.

"And if I tackle the cottage and renovations but he doesn't plan a spectacular party, what happens?"

"If you succeed and Silas fails, you will be the sole owner of the house and still get your money," Carter said.

She would have to learn as much as she could about Silas and use it against him so she could win this ridiculous contest.

"What if we both succeed?" she said.

"Then you both own the house, the two buildings, and the property equally. You also get the lump sum because you were her sister's granddaughter."

Silas took the paper wrapping that had covered the straw and twisted it around his finger. "Let me see if I get this straight. I have three weeks to plan the party. Alone. If I do it, even if she completes her end, she can't sell the house without me. Is that right?"

"That's the long and short of it."

"I won't stand by and allow her to sell that house to some corporation. We don't want businesses like that in Candlewood Falls." He pushed out of his chair. The legs scraped against the floor.

She stood too, but still had to tilt her chin to meet his gaze. "I don't want that house. I'll fix it and clean out the cottage, but I won't keep it. You can't make me."

"Seems like I can. As long as I plan that party, worst-case scenario I own half the house. If you screw up, then I own the whole thing. I won't ever sell if it means a business will take it over."

"The stipulations don't seem fair," she said. "He has less to worry about than I do."

"You don't know Silas," Carter said.

"Hey, now."

"The other thing you need to know is Georgette paid the escrow through the calendar year. She wanted the two of you to complete her request without having to worry about anything else. Whatever the house needs will be taken care of." Carter tapped the folder as if all the answers were in there.

"I just want to make sure I'm following you. I have to take care of the renovations and clear out the stone cottage by myself in order to get the inheritance."

"That's what the man said, Sticks." Silas snickered. A man in a white t-shirt and black jeans came through the door and waved. Silas and Carter waved back. She was at a disadvantage in this town, not knowing its nuances and its unwritten rules. Or that could be to her advantage. No one had expectations for her and when she was gone, no one would care. She could do whatever it took to win without the consequences of needing approval.

"One more time for the record, Silas must plan the garden party which is to happen in three weeks. If he doesn't, the house goes to you. You must handle the renovations and the cottage in three weeks or the house goes to him and you don't get any of the money. If you both succeed, you own the house fifty-fifty. Are we all clear?"

"I'm good," Silas said.

"Yeah, me too." She would be when she owned that house outright. But she could be in town longer than expected. Even after the house was complete, she'd have to put it on the market and hope a hotel chain would be interested. She had a few prospective buyers in mind. People she had done business with over the years. If her name wasn't complete dirt in the industry, she might have a strong chance.

"Wonderful. Now, if you'll all excuse me. I have another appointment." Carter grabbed his folder, weaved through the tables, waving and saying hello to most of the patrons along the way before pushing out into the afternoon heat.

She turned to Silas and held his gaze. "There is no way I'm sticking around this town. Nor do I wish to be tied to a rude man like you for eternity. I'm going to win this competition, and then I'm going to sell that house to the highest bidder."

Without waiting for a response, she marched out of the coffeehouse with her head held high and her shoulders straight. She had dealt with men like Silas before who thought they were smarter and better than a woman. Well, she would show him. Claudia Jacobs was no one's fool.

CHAPTER FOUR

S ilas dumped the bags on the table. Georgette's guest cottage was too big with too much space for him. He wanted his two-room cabin back where he could be in the woods and clear his head.

Here, he had a full galley-style kitchen with a long counter that opened to a living space and a vaulted ceiling. If he thought about it, this was just one big room. Other than a couch, coffee table, and television stand, there really wasn't any other furniture in the room. The ceiling fan hanging from the vaulted beam wasn't so bad. In the winter, it probably dropped the heat back into the room. But a television? He hadn't owned a television in decades.

He approached the bathroom as if something would jump out. Peering around the doorway, the scent of bleach met him first. The room was simple with a white tiled floor, a shower stall, and a small sink. For once, he wouldn't have to go far in the middle of the night if he needed to use the facilities, but he also couldn't see the sky on the way.

He shook his head. It wasn't as if he didn't use toilets with plumbing. At work, he acted like everyone else, and when he paid a visit to his children or his brother Huck, he didn't struggle with the flusher or the faucets. He wasn't literally wild. He had just grown used to his simple way of life. Couldn't blame a man for liking the things he was used to.

He put the perishables into the refrigerator and glanced out the window. The guest cottage sat slightly above the swimming pool, giving him a good view to the house and his gardens.

He had never imagined staying as long as he had to work on Georgette's gardens. He had offered some help years ago and ended up sticking around. He had said it was for her, but deep down it was for him too. Working with his hands was the thing he was best at. Relationships confounded him, especially with women; technology gave him the jitters, and he preferred real-life learning to reading about it in books.

He stepped outside and let the warm air brush over his skin. Sticks was on the back patio by the house. She had swapped her spiky pink heels for flip-flops and that silly white dress for a pair of shorts and white t-shirt. Much better. She had looked like something that should be on top of a wedding cake earlier. Now she looked relaxed.

She sat back on the lounge chair and turned up her face to the sun for a brief moment. Her eyes were closed, but he remembered they were as dark as coal. A smile played across her lips now. She hadn't smiled at all when they were in the Green Bean. Her light hair fell in thick waves over her slender shoulders. She had barely come up to his chest when she stood, but that didn't stop her from throwing fire at him with her impatient words. That was a woman who didn't roll over easily. He had half expected her to poke a finger in his chest when she had given him hell.

He had deserved it too. Well, maybe not quite as bad as she had delivered, but he saw her coming a mile away and wanted her to know it. Women like her didn't hide how they felt about things. She was used to having her way and people doing as she asked. He only had to look at her clothes to know that much.

She dropped a floppy straw hat onto her head, then added oversized sunglasses. Too bad. She had pretty eyes and boy, oh boy, did they light up when she got mad.

Her hellcat response to him loosened something in his belly that had been dormant for a long time, throwing him off guard. From the minute he had eyed her at the table with Carter, he had her sized up. Fancy clothes and jewelry. Smug smile and a distasteful glare at any mention of Georgette or this town. City girl. Had to be. But there was something else underneath all that wrapping that she was doing her level best to hide. Well, not his problem. He'd plan his party and get his house. Let someone else deal with her. And if she had a man in her life, then hats off to that guy.

At least, after he won, he would be able to make sure that the mansion and the property went into the hands of the right kind of people. He didn't want to see some bulldozer come through here, tearing everything up including his flowers. He wanted to do what was best for the house and the town.

He went back inside, leaving Sticks to her sunbathing. The indoor space was refreshing from the air-conditioning. Another modern convenience he claimed he didn't want in his house, but was nice to be around once in a while. Getting older made the heat harder to deal with at times and at night, he wouldn't mind an easier, cooler sleep.

Carter had given him Georgette's information on the garden party. The folder was four inches thick, filled with lists and notes about who to hire and who to invite, who to ask for money from, and which flowers were to be featured. He knew nothing about throwing a party. He didn't even like going to parties and rarely attended one. And if by some chance he found himself at a crowded gathering, he located the nearest door and took off at the first opportunity. If anyone other than Georgette—or his children—had asked him to organize a social gathering it would have been a flat-out no.

He couldn't allow Sticks to sell that house to anyone that operated as a corporation. So, he flipped open the folder and stared at the top page before closing it again. Tomorrow he would begin digging through everything in the folder.

"What were you up to, old lady, pairing Sticks and me together?" he said to the empty room. He couldn't predict Georgette's behavior when she was alive. One second she would rescue a puppy and the next she would call the police on a barking dog. But she always loved her garden and how he took care of it. She had become a bit of a second mother to him after his had died. A bristly mother with a bite, but a mother nonetheless.

His job was easier than his co-owner's. He had seen the inside of that cottage. A laugh bubbled in his throat. Would serve the city girl right when she discovered the mess. He went to the window again.

She still reclined on the lounge as if the whole world would do her bidding. She probably never worked hard a day in her life. Probably had married a billionaire, spent his money faster than he could make it, and then sent him to an early grave.

Carter had mentioned that Claudia Jacobs from Chicago had arrived in Candlewood Falls with nothing more than her assistant and several bags of luggage. He could safely assume there was no Mr. Jacobs. Sticks was his problem for the next three weeks. The end couldn't come fast enough.

Brad expected him soon for dinner. He took a glance at that glass shower and hesitated. A quick wash to get the day's dirt off him would be good. The pristine enclosure was too fancy for his blood, but the water pressure was probably pretty good.

Georgette had an outdoor shower by the pool. The afternoon sun had raised the heat plenty high enough for him to clean off outside. He grabbed a towel, a bar of soap, and let himself back out.

Her head pounded. Claudia allowed herself thirty minutes sitting outside in the fresh air before she would cave to the responsibilities and the headache. She didn't want to be inside. The house was too big for her alone with its long hallways and high ceilings. Ironic, since she had lived in a hotel prior to this with its high ceilings and long hallways. But there had been people around at all times. She had never been without company. Though she had certainly been alone.

When she had returned from the coffeehouse, sweating once again, she had ripped off that tulle dress, giving it back to the velvet hanger, and kicked her shoes into the closet. She would've walked around in her bra and underwear all afternoon, but the patio and the pretty garden with its rainbow of color had called to her.

Better to be outside. The house had baked unevenly like an uncalibrated oven, making some rooms too warm and too cool. The air-conditioning—though central—wasn't in great shape. That would need to be fixed, and she would put it on her list after her head let up some.

Or she could forgo the entire adventure. She wasn't viewing it as much of an adventure at the moment anyway. She hadn't planned on sharing the house with a surly man or being at his mercy as to whether or not she got the inheritance. Sure, she needed money, but she had survived with next to nothing before. She could do it again. Never mind she had been in her twenties the last time she lived in her car. She'd put a call into Carter and let him know she was out.

Swinging her legs over the side of the chaise, confident in her new decision, she soaked in the view. Bright-green landscape rolled out before her like a lush carpet. From the back patio, the property sloped down to the aquamarine pool and up to that stone cottage on her left. Flowers bloomed in bright colors all along the edges of the stone walkway and up the stone steps to the cottage.

She hadn't looked inside the cottage yet, but now that she had decided to forgo the inheritance, there didn't seem to be a point. It was a cute building up on the hill and would make for an adorable writer's cottage maybe. She could imagine renting that out, assuming it had a bathroom, to an author looking to get away and finish that nagging novel.

She had rented plenty of hotel rooms to writers and writer groups trying to make magic on the page. A cute little space like that one would rent out without any effort. A nice additional source of income and if the mansion did become a boutique hotel, the guest in the cottage would have full access, as well as to the pool and the tennis court at the back of the property. Her mind tripped over ideas, but she needed to shelve them. She wasn't staying.

Large planters filled with more flowers outlined the pool area. None of which she knew the names of. But their colors were vibrant and their fragrance lusty. The dense smell turned her stomach a little because of the headache. This place and this town weren't the city with its straight lines, glass and steel, but Georgette's home was warm and welcoming. She had to give the old girl that much.

This move was always going to be temporary. The plan had been to sell the house, get another job and move on. The quick jump from Chicago to Candlewood Falls and then on again was how she had convinced Talbot to agree to come with her. Talbot would be fine with the new decision to forgo the competition and walk away.

And if Talbot wanted to stay behind in Candlewood Falls, Claudia would understand and do whatever she could to help her friend.

Another opportunity would present itself. Claudia still had a spark left. Bright enough for someone to notice. She could go to New York this time. She had a few contacts there. Someone would give her a job if what she had done to save Louisa hadn't spread that far.

And she would do it all again even if it meant landing in Candlewood Falls and strapped with this house. No one would take advantage of a woman while she was around to see it.

Her headache would not quit. She didn't have any ibuprofen inside. Either she would have to go get some or settle for a cold soda in the refrigerator and hope the caffeine would do the trick.

Inside or not? She turned to look at the house. At least from the back it didn't glare at her. The expansive windows on this side were actually lovely. Decision made. More outside.

She took the path to the pool where the crystal-blue water invited her. Her mind jumped to the blue eyes belonging to her new nemesis. Such a shame a man that handsome was a pill and a half. She stuck her feet in the cool water. Maybe it would help her head some. Or not.

"Going for a swim?" A deep male voice startled her.

She wobbled on the pool's top plaster step, waving her hands to keep from falling in the water. Her gaze sought the source of the question and landed on a man in the outdoor shower. She hadn't noticed the shower before because of the ivy covering its side and blending it in with the other landscaping.

But she didn't miss the shoulders and head sticking out of the top now that she'd seen him. Drops of water ran down his face and dripped off his chin. If a drenched rugged man wasn't sexy before... Silas turned off the water and grabbed the towel thrown over the side of the shower.

He was naked behind that flimsy wood. Heat climbed up her cheeks. If she could with any dignity, she'd make a run for it. But hightailing it out of there now would only give him the upper hand. She stayed.

"I wanted to test the water." That was the dumbest response she could've come up with. But his appearance had thrown her. She didn't want him thinking she had walked down here to see him.

"How is it?" He wriggled from side to side, then bent and stood again. A flash of yellow towel rose and dove with each of his movements.

She took a deep breath to pull herself together and force her thoughts away from a naked man drying himself. "Wait a second. What are you doing here? Carter said no one lived here except Georgette."

"I'm bunking in the guesthouse for now." He opened the shower door.

She averted her gaze, as if she were never more interested in the flowers. "You can't stay on the property while I'm here."

"I think I can. We own this place together. Don't worry. I'll leave you to the mansion. That seems more like your kind of place. And I'll stay out here."

"What does that mean?" Her gaze betrayed her or maybe it was her damn curiosity, but she stole a look.

Silas stood there with the towel wrapped around his

trim waist, stopping above his knees, revealing toned legs. His chest didn't bulge with testosterone, but he was in great shape. White hairs mixed with darker ones, like a good spice, dusted his pecs and ran into a trail leading to that towel. As a young man, he would've been irresistible. Though, age had been good to him. Maybe better, molding him like a vintage piece of leather with healed scars and scratches.

"I'll stay on my side of the property. We won't even notice each other," he said, ignoring her question.

"You didn't answer me. What makes you think you know me so well?" No matter how attractive he was, he wedged himself under her skin like a splinter. It would take no time at all for his good looks to vanish with that snarly personality of his.

"I don't know you at all. From the looks of you and that giant ring on your finger, I'm guessing you appreciate the nicer things. That big old house is more your speed than mine, is all."

She stole a glance at her finger and hid her hand behind her back. Yes, the diamond on her finger was large and expensive. It caught the light so brilliantly that a thousand prisms exploded from its surface. But it wasn't real. It was lab made, and no one knew it.

"Why are you staying here?" She would be giving Carter River an earful when she got a hold of him. He had assured her no one would be here but her. And now a naked man stood poolside.

"A tree took its anger out on my house. Can't stay there. This place was available." He hitched his thumb over his shoulder toward the guesthouse.

She hoped the towel stayed in place. "Well, you can't stay here either. I don't want to see you every day."

"Not up to you. Georgette left us both the house. I'm staying. You can leave. You want to anyway. Might as well go now and get it over with."

She marched up to him, clearing the space between them and giving herself some of her height back now that she wasn't standing on the pool step. He still had almost a foot on her. Tilting her chin, she looked up at him.

"I'm not going anywhere. In fact, I'm going to clear out that little cottage by the end of the three weeks and you will be giving me your half of the house. Then I will sell it to the first buyer." So much for her decision to leave. She couldn't let Silas get away with implying she was the problem in this equation.

"Not likely. I'm going to plan that garden party like it's never been done before. And then you will have to give me your half of the house." He adjusted the towel on his hips.

"No matter what you say, you don't want to own this money drain any more than I do." She begged her gaze to stay on his face and not drop to anything lower.

"But I'll make sure it stays in the hands of a local person who will keep it the way it was meant to be. Gardens and all."

"Who takes care of the gardens?" She took a step back.

He crossed his arms over his chest. "I do. I've spent years here helping Georgette in the yard."

"Why does the back look like something out of a magazine and the front yard like a horror movie?"

"Georgette was a unique woman. She wouldn't let me

touch the front that often. Said she wanted the gossips in town to have something to chew on. When she wasn't paying attention, I'd run a lawn mower over it."

"You do all of this by yourself?"

"A landscaper handles the grass. My hands grow and coax these flowers to their full worth."

"That was very nice of you." She meant that, but bit back the part where she said Georgette probably didn't appreciate it. "Don't go getting too comfortable here. I'll have that cottage cleared and those renos done in no time."

Now she knew he had a vested interest in the garden. He might fight harder to keep what he had created. Anyone standing on the property could see how much attention went into everything around them. He cared— a lot. And that piece of information was in her arsenal.

"Try all you want, but you won't get that space cleared out by next year, never mind three weeks. And I'm rooted in this town. I can wait you out for the next twenty years if I have to. I don't need the money."

"You're too old to wait twenty years." She only said that because he had hit too close to home about the money thing. She had given herself away earlier today, and she didn't like giving up her vulnerabilities. They were often used against her.

"Who told you my age?" He leaned down toward her. A glimmer twinkled in his eyes. A hint of soap tickled her nose.

"I can guess." She swallowed the rest of what she was going to say. Something along the lines of the wrinkles in his skin, but that was below the belt and honestly, only made him better-looking.

"Guess how?" He arched a brow.

"Your eyes. Your eyes say you're old." She hadn't swallowed hard enough, apparently.

He stepped back again, his lips pressing into a thin line. Without another word, he turned on his bare heel and left her standing there alone, struggling under the weight of her guilt.

"You really need to learn to keep your mouth shut," she said under her breath.

But the man was incorrigible with all his implications that she was a snob. He had made a decision based on her outward appearance only. Oh, who was she kidding? That was what she always wanted—people to size her up and decide she was wealthy and important. Why did it bother her now?

She too turned on her heel and marched toward the house, pulling the back glass door open and nearly colliding with Talbot. They both stopped short.

"What are you doing here?" she said with more vinegar than she meant to accent with.

"Nice to see you too." Talbot stepped aside. Her long light-brown hair was pulled back. She exuded casual with her black tunic top, trendy jeans, and strappy sandals.

For years, she and Talbot had traded fashion tips for work and play. Claudia often video called her to get another opinion about a new outfit. That was how their friendship had formed.

"I'm sorry. It's been a rough day. I didn't expect to see you until tomorrow. Do you want a drink?" She weaved her way through the piano room with its stone floor—stone was everywhere in this house—and into the kitchen that would need updating at some point. But not by her, if she could help it.

"I'll take a glass of wine if you have it in this old place." Talbot slid onto the chair at the wood kitchen table.

She found a bottle of wine in the smaller of the two refrigerators. Aunt Georgette must've used it as a beverage refrigerator because the only thing in it was bottles of wine, a couple of cans of beer, and a seltzer. She rummaged around in the drawers, opening and closing all of them until she discovered a bottle opener in the last one by the sink.

Wineglasses were easier to locate. Aunt Georgette had one cabinet with glass doors. The glasses were on full display. The crystal was heavy and cut. She doubted they were cut glass. Her aunt had good taste in crystal. And wine. This bottle was a cabernet sauvignon from the early nineties.

"My aunt left all of her personal items around the house, including a pantry full of canned food, boxes of cereal, and for extra fun half-eaten bags of pretzels." She poured and handed the glass to Talbot.

"Yuck. How soon can you have the house up for sale?"

She poured a glass for herself, then thought better of it. Wine would tighten the viselike grip causing her headache. She'd like to blame the pain on Silas, but it had more to do with the humidity and the stress. She grabbed the diet cola in the big fridge instead.

"Here's the thing." She sat opposite Talbot and told her about the day she'd had, including the part where she had found Silas in the shower.

"At least he was nice to look at. You could've found something you'd never be able to unsee out there. If you get me." Talbot raised her glass in a toast.

"Oh, I do." And she did not need that kind of visual. Silas was easy on the eyes. He did have that much going for him.

"I hate to bring up reality, but you need another hotel to work for when this is all over." Talbot adjusted her collar.

"I'll get something. We can look in New York. I'm not staying in this town. Forget the competition."

"You aren't going to allow Silas Wilde to win this competition." Talbot tugged on her shirt again.

"I don't want the house." She never wanted the house. She wanted security. Peace of mind.

"No, you want the money._And you need the money. Don't walk away from this, Claudia. You can win." Talbot downed her wine and jumped up to pour more.

"But we're going to be here longer than we thought and that's not fair to you."

"You have three weeks to take care of business. I can find something to do for three weeks. Is it warm in here?" Talbot's cheeks flushed pink. She grabbed a piece of old mail from the counter and fanned herself.

"Not really. Are you okay?"

"Just a little frazzled with the move."

"I'm sorry if I was selfish in asking you to stay with me. You should do what's best for you no matter what that is. Work for someone else, start a new career anything." She had asked too much of her longtime friend and colleague by coming to this small town with no opportunities.

"I'm not leaving you. We're a team and that's how it stays." Talbot filled her wine glass with water from the tap and downed that too.

"Are you sure you're okay?"

"I'm good. Just tired. I had to relocate a ton of junk from that house I'm renting. The previous tenant collected things from garage sales. I mean, a ton of things. Some of it is cute, but there's so much. I couldn't look at it all and started moving it to the garage."

"I'll come over and help you."

"No, you stay here and deal with the shower guy and this house." Talbot waved the piece of mail in the air. "And by the way, what's best for me is to stick it out with my good friend. I'll put out some feelers in New York. Hopefully, your name isn't completely tarnished."

"I'm realistic. I pissed off a very wealthy, very influential man who had the power to fire me and spread rumors about my sanity and reliability. Everyone in the premiere hotel business could know by now that I'm a liability."

"If they believe that, they don't know the truth." Talbot squeezed her hand.

"The truth is sometimes relative." She turned the sweaty soda can in circles and drifted away from Aunt Georgette's kitchen back to the day she had accidentally walked into a hotel room that should have been empty. Instead of an unmade bed, bath towels littering the floor, and the stench of stale body odor, she had stumbled upon Louisa, her housekeeping uniform askew, pointing a steak knife from the room service cart at a fully aroused guest in his underwear.

Louisa had said the guest harassed her. The powerful

businessman said otherwise. It had become of game of his word against hers. In the end, his say had been bigger, louder, and filled with more dollars. Claudia and Louisa were handed their walking papers. Louisa had wanted to apologize to the guest in order to keep her job, but Claudia had convinced her not to. Afterward, Louisa had decided that she didn't need a friend like Claudia. That, unfortunately, was sometimes life in the big city.

"If New York is a bust, we'll try Dallas or Atlanta. Or hell, we'll totally reinvent ourselves. How does that sound?" Talbot smiled, but it didn't reach her eyes.

Something was bothering her friend, but Talbot would not say until she was ready. Claudia had learned a long time ago to give Talbot the space she needed and when she was ready, she would spill like a tilted jar of marbles.

"I don't know how to be anyone else." She had worked so hard to be who she was and not the poor girl whose mother couldn't afford to feed them some days or the terrified little girl living next door to monsters. Or the young woman in housekeeping fighting off unwanted advances.

Who could she possibly become now?

"Forget that idea. Besides, I like you just the way you are, Claudia, queen of the high heels. So, how do you plan on beating your mountain man?"

She could imagine Silas on horseback, riding up a mountain at sunset. Or hiking up a mountain with a shotgun strapped to his back, in case a bear approached.

"He's not my anything. I'm going to have to hit him hard. That garden party can't happen."

"I don't like that look in your eye. You're up to something."

"You know my philosophy. Do whatever it takes. And if I'm sticking around to win, then that's what I'll do." Targeting the flowers would give her the advantage. They were his weak spot and without them, that party would fail. No one would come to a garden party without a garden.

"Be careful, Claudia. I don't want to see you hurt again."

"I won't get hurt. I have nothing to lose, except the money. And yes, I need it, but if for some small reason I don't win, I'll dust myself off and start again. I'm not emotionally invested here. Not like Chicago." Chicago had wrapped around her whole life, seeping inside the crevices until she would never be completely free of it.

"Are you declaring some kind of war?"

"Not war. Just making sure he doesn't win."

Talbot poured another glass of wine. "You know, declaring a little love might do you some good."

"With whom? Silas Wilde? What for?"

"You said he was hot in that towel. And it's been a while since you've had a male companion."

She hopped out of her seat and darted across the room, as if Talbot's idea had climbed into her shorts and bit her. "Oh, please. I don't need a man. And I'm not looking for love or sex. Especially not from Silas Wilde."

CHAPTER FIVE

Claudia scoured the internet for an excavator. It shouldn't be so hard to find one. They were in New Jersey after all. The state was hardly a third-world country even if Candlewood Falls reminded her of Mayberry.

She was grateful for the Wi-Fi access already in place at Georgette's oversized house. The connection didn't reach far, but she didn't mind sitting at the kitchen table where the router was only feet away and tucked into a cove. The long windows provided an extra dose of light and the view of the expansive garden. In fact, right now, Silas meandered through the garden checking and rechecking the flowers. For what, she had no idea.

Guests would love to have a cup of coffee here each morning as the sun slipped into the sky. After breakfast, they could enjoy lunch on the patio and dinner in the large dining room.

What was she doing, trying to picture this place as a boutique hotel? She wouldn't be here to make that happen, and she cared not at all about what the next owners did with this place. All she needed to do was get the house ready to sell and win the competition. She would, however, need a second router for upstairs in the bedroom. On tomorrow's list.

"Knock, knock."

She dragged her gaze to the wide-open entryway, leading to the foyer. Van waited with a smile on his face and a toolbelt around his jean-clad waist. What had he said his last name was? *Wilde*. Another one. How many were there in this town? Silas probably had a huge family, something she had always longed for.

"Hi, Van. Is everything okay?"

"I found something you should see."

"Can it wait?" She really wanted to book the excavator. This may be the worst thing she had ever done in her life, but she was going to win this contest, since that's what it was at its core. Silas didn't care about owning this house anyway. He only cared about stopping her from selling it to a corporation. If the flowers had to go, then they did. Maybe this was a bit of a war declaration.

"Not really. It's going to put a bit of a delay in some of the renovations. We can't go much further until it's fixed."

Reluctantly, she shut the computer and followed Van. He led her to the south side of the house which had once acted as servant quarters. The décor changed from wood and paneling to a black-and-white-tiled floor and yellow walls. Sterile.

He took the staircase down into the basement. A damp, musty smell hit her first. She pulled her shirt up over her nose. The floor was made of dirt, and years of black grime covered the cinderblock foundation. Two floodlights pointed to the bottom of one wall.

"You have black mold." Van squatted down and pointed to a small area.

"Are you sure?"

"Well, not entirely. We have to send out a sample to be tested. If it is, we could be faced with lifting the house and putting in a new foundation. If it's plain old mold, then we'll get rid of it. But we don't want to do anything to kick it up if it's black mold. Sanding and painting and repairing any cracks have to wait."

Wait? She didn't have time to wait. Three weeks was hardly a lot of time to buff this house into shape. "How long for the test results?"

"Dean said he'll ask for a rush. He's got a few contacts." Van stood and adjusted his belt.

"Do I have to move out?" She had nowhere to go, unless Talbot would let her bunk with her.

"Not yet. I advise you not to come down here, though."

"No worries there." She didn't wait for Van, but turned for the steps. She needed fresh air and sunshine instead of mold and gloom. This problem could set her back weeks. Or worse. She definitely needed to put a stop to Silas now so he couldn't get ahead of her.

She pulled a bottled water from the fridge and offered one to Van. He shook his head. "Van, are you related to Silas Wilde?"

"He's my father's brother. There's five of them. Well, there was. My uncle SJ died a long time ago. I was about twenty-four when that happened."

"I'm sorry to hear that." The Wildes were a big family

then. Did all the brothers have children? How many more would she bump into in this town?

Talbot could be right about the dangers of tangling with Silas, but not for the reasons she had thought. A man with a large family would have a lot of people in his corner, willing to help him in any way they could.

"Thanks."

"Are you all close?" She hoped she sounded casual as she sipped her water, letting her gaze wander to the windows and away from Van. As if she couldn't care less about his answer.

"Pretty close. I guess. Most of us live in town. How do you know my uncle? He prefers to keep to himself. Meeting new people isn't exactly his thing."

"I met him. I'm sure word will get around in a town like this, but he's staying in the guesthouse out back."

"Right. I had heard about the problems with his place. I'll let you know what Dean finds out about the mold. I'm going to head out unless you need something else."

"I don't think so. You know more about the renovations than I do." Only because she wasn't taking the time to get involved. She had overseen renovations at The Barry Watson plenty of times. When no one was looking, she even could handle a tape measure and a hammer.

"See you then."

She waited until the click of the unhappy front door echoed in the foyer before returning to her task of investigating the excavator.

"Don't do it," she whispered under her breath and turned her gaze back to the garden. Silas was gone, but those flowers seemed to reach for the sun with arms wide open, all too happy to decorate the yard like confetti.

She had to win. She had no choice. Silas could not get that garden party off or she would lose her last chance to save herself.

All her other aces were used up. Most of her connections had stopped taking her calls. Whether she liked it or not, she wasn't getting any younger. In her mind, she was still thirty-five, but her body only laughed at that idea and reminded her often that thirty-five was gone from the rearview mirror.

She could almost picture settling down to a quiet life instead of battling the ideals of a major corporation that only cared about the bottom line and how many hotel rooms were occupied. Let someone younger with ideal-istic expectations run a premiere hotel. But what would she have, if she didn't have work? The answer paralyzed her. Her work defined her. She would be nothing with-out it.

Her internet search proved fruitful. An excavator was available for large jobs, and all she had to do was reserve it online. Her luck had finally turned.

Silas turned off the chainsaw. His arms vibrated up to his elbows, and sweat ran down his face and the back of his neck, soaking the collar of his t-shirt. He used the hem to wipe his face. The morning had heated up plenty fine. That sun would cook his skin in another hour, and he still hadn't cut away enough branches from the tree resting on his house.

His back complained about the hard work that usually suited him. He should hire someone to come out here and take care of things instead of battling this tree alone.

That nice kid, Drew, who cut Georgette's grass, could probably have a crew out here and the whole thing hauled away in no time. But he wanted to clear most of the tree himself, if only to prove he still could.

He hadn't bothered to tell anyone his plan to cut away as much of the tree as possible. In fact, he had lied to Brad and Lyra the other night, claiming he had called someone when they had asked how the removal was coming along. If Brad knew what he was up to, he'd be here with the entire picking crew from the orchard. And Silas wanted nothing to do with being taken care of by his son or his team. He appreciated that his son wanted to, but he wasn't so old he needed tending to.

An engine's growl echoed in the short distance. Someone must have turned off the road and came his way. He wasn't expecting anyone and rarely received guests. Which was the way he preferred it. It wasn't as if he didn't like people entirely. He just wanted to have more than enough space to breathe in. Living in town suffocated him a little.

That new neighbor of his was going to squeeze every bit of air from him. She had a bite to her tongue and a glint in her eye that he liked putting there. Give him a feisty woman any day. Just not one wearing glitter. He wanted a woman who would swing an axe beside him and not mind the work.

A faded green pickup bounced along the dirt drive and parked beside his truck. A bluesy song drifted out the window on a growling guitar riff. The engine clicked off and so did the song about a woman robbing your soul.

Silas' brother Huck unfolded from the driver's side, the door creaking on old hinges. Huck offered a short wave and a thin smile.

"Looks like you could use a little help," Huck said, shielding his eyes. His brother was two years older than him with a head of white hair and a stomach straining against the buttons of his shirt. Huck lumbered over with his bow legs and slow stride.

"Who said I needed any help?" He put the chainsaw down to give his hands a break and wiped them on his pants. He was glad to see Huck if only for the distraction from the work.

"No one said it. I can see it." Huck saddled up next to him and wiped his face with a handkerchief he pulled from his front jeans pocket.

"I'm doing just fine. I don't need any help."

"It's too damn hot to be doing this." Huck eyed the tree still full of obstinate branches and the small pile Silas had cut. He couldn't hide the small dent he made in the work.

"Heat's not bothering me." A tall glass of iced tea would be nice, but he forgot to bring some. Rookie mistake, but he had been in a hurry to get out of that guesthouse before he bumped into Claudia again.

When she had spied him in the shower, he hadn't known which way to turn and was thankful for the walls to hide him, standing there in his altogether. Then he figured, what the hell, let her see him in a towel. He had nothing to hide.

"I thought you would say something dumb like the heat isn't getting to you. But you can't do this alone. You're too old." Huck shoved the handkerchief back in his pocket.

"You're older than me."

"I'm in better shape." Huck choked out a laugh and slapped him on the shoulder.

He let a good laugh go too and it was almost as refreshing as the iced tea would be. Almost. "Any chance you brought your chainsaw?"

"Of course, I did. Do you think I was born yesterday?"

"I do. And at night." Being in a family with four other brothers was never easy. Too many personalities and egos banging into each other around every turn. But no matter what problems they may have, he could always count on Huck to be his big brother, lending a hand. Those times he was grateful for the size of the Wilde clan.

"Ah. You're not even funny." Huck waved him and his dumb joke away.

They worked side by side for what felt like the whole afternoon, but what had actually only been an hour. His arms ached, and his shoulders burned. He might have to consider taking a swim in that pool over at Georgette's to loosen the muscles a little and maybe get another glimpse at Sticks and her pretty legs.

He didn't need thoughts of that woman while he was operating machinery. She might be pretty, but he could smell the trouble she would bring. He needed to keep his head on straight and plan that party in enough time that he remained half-owner of the house so she couldn't sell it to a corporation that would ruin his town.

Huck offered him a bottled water from the cooler he also thought to bring. Huck poured half of it over his head and then drank the other in one gulp.

"Are you seriously going to plan a flower party?" Huck said.

"Brad told you. I asked him not to say anything yet." Another problem with a large family was the amount of people's lips spilling secrets.

"Not Brad. Alvarez told me."

Raf was like a second son to him. Couldn't get mad at Raf any more than he would if it had been Brad.

"It's a garden party. There's a difference." He should've known the news of him planning any party at all would rip through their family in record speed. An article in the local paper was probably already in the works.

"Gardens are for vegetables and fruits. I don't see you as a party planner. Is someone going to help you?"

"I don't need any. I don't think anyway. I'll make some calls. Hire back all the people Georgette used and that should be that. I've got it under control." More than he did his living arrangements. Sure, he had a place to hang his hat, but he had a lot of work to get his home back in order.

He needed to talk about something else and decided to be the one asking questions that might not want to be answered.

"Are you warming up to Raf any?" he said, glancing over his water bottle to wait for Huck's reaction.

Raf Alvarez was engaged to Huck's middle daughter

Ember. At the beginning of their relationship, Huck had stuck his big mouth where it didn't belong, nearly ruining the whole thing.

"He's okay enough. Treats my girl good. She's happy. A father can't ask for more than that, can he?"

"Not at all." He agreed wholeheartedly since Brooklyn was living the kind of life he had always wanted for her. That wasn't always the case. Knowing his little girl, who wasn't little at all, went to bed safe and sound each night was a relief for him.

"I like Raf. Always have. Don't give him grief. He outranks you." That was the standing joke around the orchard since Raf was Brad's second-in-command. It usually got the expected rise out of Huck.

"Careful, my hands are getting shaky with this saw." But Huck barked out another laugh.

Huck cared a lot about titles and their last name. He had been known in his years to throw both around without any thought as to who he hit with them. For more years than Silas cared to think about, Huck acted like an ornery old fool. Only after Huck's wife became ill and passed did Huck soften and become the kind of man Silas knew he was.

Silas had never paid much attention to titles. Didn't even care that his name was on the sign outside the orchard. He had an ancestor somewhere far enough back that he never met who had put that sign up. Had little to do with him. He loved the land, the trees, and the family he knew. That was all.

From when they were kids, Huck always looked out for him. Silas preferred to stay quiet. Not Huck. Huck would take on a fight with anyone who asked and plenty who hadn't. And if anyone had even tried to push him around or bother him at school, it was his brother Huck who stepped in and put a stop to it.

The years had hardened Huck. He was glad some of that hardness had worn away.

"What about the guest list?" Huck said, dragging his thoughts back to the present and the hot sun cracking the dirt under his boots.

"Guest list?"

"You have to invite people to the party, Silas. Did you think about that?" Huck gathered some of the branches into a pile out of the way.

He hadn't given guests a thought. He had never even attended that garden party for all the years Georgette held it. She would yell at him each and every time, telling him he needed to show up because he was the one who kept her flowers in top shape. She always tried the guilt approach too, saying his mother would want him there. His mother had wanted no such thing. She had been the first one to tell him to live his life his way.

"I'll figure it out." A list must exist in that folder of papers.

"You're too stubborn to ask for help. Just like today. But you might be in over your head with the tiny details and whatnot. I know Brooklyn is busy with the new baby and Brad knows as little about parties as you do, but Ember and Petra are around. I'm sure your boy's lady would help you too. She's crafty, isn't she?"

"Lyra. Try and remember her name, huh?" Lyra was very creative. She had decorated her and Brad's house with things he would never imagine as art. She had a habit of finding unique things in dumpsters. He wasn't one to judge, and Lyra put a smile on Brad's face. Again, a father couldn't ask for more.

"Lyra. I know her name. It just slipped my mind. Well, will you ask one of the girls? Or Sam. Sam can plan a party."

Their nephew Sam, SJ's boy, was a good kid even though he wasn't any more a kid than any of their kids. He would always think of his brothers' children as kids. Sam's heart was as big as the tree on his cabin. He would jump to help any of them, if asked.

"I don't need any help, and I don't want the likes of all of you hanging around me while I do it. It's a party. How hard can it be to plan? My house here is more of a problem." Georgette's notes were confusing. He couldn't make out which way was up and had abandoned his last two attempts to figure it out. Like he had said, it was a party. How hard could it be?

"This mess here needs a tree guy and a bulldozer. Aren't you ready to come in from the woods yet? You proved your point."

"I wasn't trying to prove a point. I like living this way."

"I know you do. All I'm saying is, it wouldn't hurt to take a leak indoors in the middle of the night when the temps are freezing. You can't like having to drop your drawers in twenty degrees."

He didn't. But bathroom breaks in the middle of the night weren't all the time. And he had ways to deal with that problem if there was a storm going on and he couldn't go outside. He couldn't lie that last night at the strike of two in the morning when nature called he was grateful for the short walk to the other room and the flush of a toilet. Moving inside permanently would say something and he didn't want anyone hearing the wrong things.

"How about we grab some lunch in town? My treat." He was done talking about the party and his way of living. Plus, he was starving from all the work, and he wanted to get in out of the sun for a bit.

"Sounds good to me. Murphy's for a burger?" Huck wiped his hands on his pants.

"Should we clean up first?"

"Hell, no. We're Wildes. If someone doesn't like our stink, too bad." Huck threw his head back and boomed an explosive laugh.

Yeah, that was the brother he knew and loved. And Silas was grateful he had come by to help him. But he would reserve the praise. Huck wasn't the emotional type, and Silas didn't want that head to grow any bigger.

He could use a quick shower because the stench of sweat drying on his skin was almost too much for him, but Huck was right about not caring. It wasn't as if he had anyone to impress.

CHAPTER SIX

Burger juices dripped off her chin. Claudia wiped her face and refrained from licking her fingers in public. Every once in a while she threw caution to the wind and ate a fat hamburger and fries. Today was one of those days.

She couldn't get a burger like this one in any city she had been in. Next, she would have to try a pizzeria. New York and New Jersey had the best pizza, if she didn't count the deep-dish brick oven pizza from Chicago.

Renovations were at a standstill while the mold was tested. Paneling needed to be torn out and drywall put in its place in several of the downstairs rooms, but it couldn't now. Upgrades were needed to the electricity and the plumbing. Something about copper. She couldn't remember what at the moment. If work wasn't being done on the house, and messing with her goals to win, she might as well get herself a satisfying lunch.

Eating alone hadn't bothered her a long time ago. Somewhere around fifty she stopped giving a damn about a lot of things. She relished sitting in a restaurant like Murphy's with its low ceiling, shadowy corners, and long bar, as she watched the patrons. She always made up stories about the people and could entertain herself for hours.

After lunch she planned on checking out the stone cottage. She had avoided it until now and couldn't put it off any longer. The clock was ticking, as they said. Whoever they were. For now, she would sit and eat cow.

Light filtered in, pushing the darkness aside as the door swung open on a whoosh. Two men at the bar turned in the direction of the light and then back to their half-empty glasses in front of them, unfazed by what they saw. She followed their dull gazes.

And almost choked on her burger.

Silas ambled in as if he were in no rush. He stood tall, his shoulders back. A smile tugged on those sexy lips, igniting the creases around his eyes. His clothes were covered in dust or dirt, but he either didn't care or didn't notice. Another man who bore a strong resemblance to him followed. They waved to the man behind the bar and took a seat closer to the door.

Thankfully, he hadn't noticed her sitting in the corner. Looked as if her lunch was over. She would get the rest of her burger to go and finish it on the back patio at the mansion that was quickly becoming one of her favorite places in the house. Probably because the mold couldn't get her there.

She signaled for a waitress. The woman helping her earlier had seemed to disappear.

"Can I get you something?" the waitress said with an infectious smile. Her name tag read Flora, the Latin of her name, meaning flower of all things. Flowers would now haunt Claudia until she could rub the memory of Candlewood Falls from her mind.

Flora was a petite woman, in denim shorts and a Murphy's t-shirt, sporting a thin shape that no matter how many squats Claudia did, she would never have those thighs. Flora's ponytail sat high on her head and bounced when she spoke.

"A box and the check, please."

Flora produced the bill from her apron and placed it on the table. "I'll be right back with that box." She hurried away, making Claudia think of a happy bunny.

She checked her phone to keep herself from staring in Silas' direction. He had chosen the chair facing her. If she stared, she risked making eye contact. If she kept her head down, she could always feign surprise if they crossed paths. Maybe he would go to the bathroom, and she could make a break for it.

No messages or emails of any importance waited for her, just junk. Chicago didn't need her anymore. No one needed her except maybe Talbot. And Talbot had kept herself busy in this new town. She was fitting in far better than Claudia.

Her heart ached. She was alone in the world, having devoted her life to work and having nothing to show for it now. Even if she hadn't burned all her bridges, who would want a fifty-four-year-old when they could have someone younger who cost less?

"Here you go." Flora's return snapped her back to the dimly lit Murphy's with its smell of grilled beef and beer hops. In addition to the box, Flora handed her a pink flyer. "I hope you don't mind me asking you. I'm asking everyone who comes into Murphy's. We're putting a meal train together for someone in town who's sick and doesn't have any help. She's truly alone."

Objections formed on her tongue in the shape of heavy straight-angled words. *No time. New in town. Not settled. Not staying.* She swallowed each one. Hadn't she just thought about how alone she was? If she were sick, who would care for her? An ugly, shriveled answer rose up in her mind.

She scanned the flyer. Not only Murphy's was helping out, but other local eateries appeared to be a part of this meal train too.

"Dining Car is a great organization," Flora said. "We help anyone who needs meals brought to them. Could be a new single mom who can't get out of the house or someone with a broken leg who struggles to navigate their stairs. Or in this case, a lovely woman who's too sick to care for herself. We have several dates left. Or you can donate, if you don't want to cook."

Unexpected tears sprang to her eyes. She dropped her gaze to her lap. She had been a child and then a young woman whose stomach had cramped with hunger. Nights filled with snacks from the vending machine had acted as her gourmet dinner. One whole summer she had practically existed on soft pretzels and canned cheese.

"Hey, Flora." A deep male voice snuck under the table and lifted her chin.

"Silas, it's great to see you in here. We miss you when you don't come around," Flora said in her sprightly voice.

Whether Claudia wanted to admit it or not, Flora was right. Silas looked good even in his dirty clothes.

Stubble dotted his strong jaw, filling in around his salt-and-pepper goatee, only adding to the rugged texture of his skin. Those blue eyes were bright beneath his dark brows and the seemingly healthy hairline.

Silas leaned down and placed a kiss on Flora's cheek. Flora scrunched up her face, squishing her eyes closed, and pulled away, waving her hand back and forth.

"You stink." Her laugh twinkled around them as if fireflies dashed from her mouth, begging to be caught.

"Sorry about that. Working outdoors today. How's the latest meal train coming along?" He inched his chin in the direction of the flyer, but ignored Claudia entirely.

Ire ran up her spine. No one ignored her. Well, no one used to ignore her. Here, in Candlewood Falls, she was nobody, a stranger.

He was probably still mad about her calling him old. Fury would've blasted out of her skull if someone had called her that. She wished she could take the thoughtless words back. Just because they were competitors, that didn't mean she should attack his person. For her, this was not personal. It was business.

"Eudora's meal train is going great. We've had plenty of people sign up to help out. And Brad's been bringing apples and donuts to Eudora every week. Brooklyn knitted a blanket for her. Such a lovely gesture. The blanket is full of dropped stitches." More fireflies twinkled out of Flora's mouth. "Brooklyn puts her heart into everything she does. Eudora loves it."

"That's my daughter." Silas' face lit up. The creases around his eyes ignited and sent shivers into her belly. His smile said a thousand things about his love for his daughter.

"Oh, I'm sorry. Where are my manners? Do you two know each other?" Flora glanced between them.

"We've met," she and Silas said at the same time.

"Wonderful. You won't find a better guy in town than Silas." Flora patted his arm. "I didn't get your name."

"Sticks," he said before she could open her mouth.

"Sticks?" Flora's eyebrows creased.

"Those ridiculous shoes she wears." Silas pointed to her feet.

Her right leg crossed over her left, her foot tapping a rapid beat to match that of her heart. Today she had slipped on a simple black sandal with a two-inch heel. Not one of her higher ones, but the heel was thin. In her mind, thin heels said sexy and confidant, but now Silas had drawn attention to them as if they were nothing more than wooden carnival stilts on her feet.

"My name is Claudia. Please don't listen to him." She shot Silas a glare. At least she hoped she did, but he only smirked in return. Whatever look crossed her face, it didn't have the effect she had hoped for.

"Oh. Well, Claudia, can we count on you?" Flora clasped her hands under her chin.

"Do you cook?" Silas arched a brow and rocked on his heels.

"Of course, I do." She didn't make a habit of it any longer because cooking for one was no fun. It was easier to order in or pick up a quick salad. "I'd be happy to help. I'll take two open dates to make Eudora meals."

Offering two dates had slipped out in a mad rush to stick it to Silas since she certainly couldn't use her heels to do the job. She had planned to say one date, maybe. A donation would be easier. A gift card even.

But prepare two meals? Did she really have time for that? And what would she make? She wasn't even sure the oven at the mansion worked. Then she would have to deliver it, and her car hadn't arrived from Chicago yet.

Tugging on the hem of her white sleeveless blouse, she pulled herself together. All her flustering had only to do with nerves. A woman was sick and alone. The least she could do was cook.

Silas regarded her with something like either suspicion or curiosity. She wasn't sure which and wasn't going to ask, but his blue eyes had smoldered. And that made her insides warm. Time to get out of Murphy's before she did something she would regret, like start to really like him.

"Sign me up for whatever dates you need." She pulled a business card and a credit card out of her wallet. "You can text me at that number. The email isn't good anymore, though."

Silas grabbed the card out of her hand.

"Hey."

"Why is the email bad?" he said.

"Because I don't work there any longer." She yanked it back and handed it to Flora.

Claudia would not go into explanation about her lack of employment to this man whose family, she had recently discovered, owned the orchard in town.

She had done a little research after her conversation in her kitchen with Talbot. She wanted to know if she could find out anything about Silas that might be useful for the competition. And okay, if she were being honest, to find out a little about him as a person.

She discovered the family owned and operated Wilde

Orchard and how it had been in Candlewood Falls for generations. She had never had the pleasure of putting down too many roots as a child.

Silas was part owner of this orchard that boasted pick-your-own apples in the fall along with his brothers, a niece, and a nephew. Further digging, because honestly she couldn't help herself, brought her to a copy of his divorce close to thirty years ago. No marriage on file. And no ring on his finger today.

"I'll take care of the bill," Flora said and bounced off. Her ponytail swung in her wake.

"Would you please excuse me?" She waved him away. His presence stole all the air in the room. Breathing seemed difficult while he stared down at her with his intense gaze.

"Why don't you work at your job anymore?" he said, instead of taking the hint and leaving.

"It's a long story. Isn't your friend waiting for you?" She pointed in the direction of the man with the white hair Silas had left at the table.

"My brother? He's fine. He has his food and a beer." Silas grabbed a fry off her plate and ate it with a wide smile, almost laughing at his playfulness.

"Seriously?" Not that she minded all that much. She wasn't going to eat any more of those fries and if he had bothered to ask like a gentleman, she would have said yes. Offering her that impish look in his eye was a bonus.

"Should I have asked first?"

"I would say so. You don't need to keep me company until my check comes." She wondered which brother had accompanied Silas to lunch today.

"Offering to make two meals was a nice thing to do. Eudora could use the help."

Flora returned with the check holder and receipt for her to sign, leaving it on the corner of the table and scooting away to help another customer.

"It's not a big deal to help someone who needs it," she said, adding a generous tip for Silas to see. A huge deal would be if she couldn't stay in the house due to the mold. Or if the electricity crapped out at the wrong time because they couldn't fix the breaker box. She would have to impose on Talbot, who wouldn't mind, but Claudia had imposed enough on her. And something still had Talbot's attention, which Claudia didn't understand, but wouldn't ask about. Talbot was a private person. When she was ready, Talbot would tell her.

Silas looked at her with warmth instead of disdain. Something she could get used to but shouldn't, considering their opposing goals. Looked like she couldn't allow word to get out that she bought a gift card after all.

"It actually is a very big deal. Especially because you're a stranger in this town. Your generosity will go a long way around here and get you accepted by the locals."

"I'm not looking to fit in. I don't plan on staying. I plan on winning our little competition and moving on to the next city." She didn't need anyone's approval. At this stage of her life, she was done caring what others thought of her. She had worked hard and done whatever she had to in order to get by. She never hurt anyone along the way, but she had only ever had herself to rely on.

Small-town living, where every person knew what

the others had done before they did, wasn't for her. She liked the anonymity of a city that blended her into the crowds and ignored her at the same time. Her life was her own, and no one else had to accept that.

"You're not going to win. I will pull that party off without a hitch, and you won't get the money you desperately want. Do you need the money for more shoes?"

She pushed out of the booth, swaying on her pointy heels, and catching a whiff of sweat, a little cedar, and a lot of male — sexy. Flora was wrong.

He gripped her elbow and arched a brow. His touch shot fire up her arm and sizzled in her chest. The room faded away while she held his gaze.

"Careful there," he said.

She tugged her arm away and the warmth flew away with it. She wanted the heat and the connection back because a chill settled over her as quickly as the heat had consumed her.

"You don't know me. You never will."

She hurried from Murphy's without a look back. It wasn't until she was a block away that she realized she had left her wallet and her credit card inside.

So much for the grand exit. She wouldn't go back and give him the satisfaction of seeing her eat crow. His assumption that she was materialistic sliced at her. Something that she had been accused of a thousand times and which had never bothered her before. She had wanted people to think she had money and came from money. Her childhood had been an embarrassment and even when she understood her mother had done her very best, allowing people to think she had always been a part of their world lined with money got her a seat at the table and a chance to be taken seriously.

But coming from Silas, for some reason she had wanted to tell the truth. Well, she had better knock off that kind of thinking.

She walked toward the red mill and the river with the sun on her back and a slight breeze in the air. A perfect summer day even if she felt anything but perfect at the moment. The waterfall roared like thunder, drowning out the noise in her head. She would wait here until Silas had a chance to finish his lunch and leave the tavern. Only then would she go back to Murphy's and retrieve her things.

She found a bench and sat. Alone. And waited.

Silas opted for the outside shower again. As long as it was sunny and warm, like it was right now, he would use it. No need to dirty up that glass enclosure for just him. He washed up, constantly glancing in the direction of the big house, hoping for a glimpse of Claudia. She was beautiful and sexy when she was fired up. He could watch her like that all day. And when she directed that fire at him, he thought about kissing her.

But she was trouble with her fancy shoes, jewelry, and penchant for money. Getting involved with a woman like that would end up in a repeat heartbreak. He had learned his lesson after his wife Patricia had left them all for a fancier life. A life he could never give her and didn't understand how she thought he would have. Women like his ex-wife and Claudia Jacobs of Chicago never took to him.

He'd stay on his side of the property, avoid her in town as much as possible, and get through the next few weeks. Right after he returned her wallet.

Cold water ran over his tired muscles that ached from using the chainsaw. He kept telling himself he needed to get his plans under way for the party. If he lost, Claudia would win the house and sell it. If he won, then she might be forced to stay in town and learn that a quiet way of life was better than her big city any day.

Her staying... why would he want that? He should let her win and let her go. But he wouldn't disrespect Georgette's last wishes even if they were the half-crazy. And the town deserved to have this property preserved the way it was. Maybe the house could become a national landmark someday, like the big marble building at the university near the shore. Georgette's house would never become a landmark if Claudia got her hooks in long enough to sell it to the highest bidder.

He turned off the water and reached for the towel. He should've left the wallet by the back door for her, or let himself in and leave it somewhere she would see it. He had a key and doubted Sticks even knew. But he had wanted to get cleaned up first. If Flora at Murphy's had said something about his stench, then he was ripe. That was probably what had Claudia weaving on her feet in front of him. Not that he minded gripping her elbow to steady her. When his hand went around her thin arm, heat ran over his skin and settled in his chest.

He should've insisted to Huck that they clean up

first. Now, Claudia had another reason to believe he was uncivilized.

No sign of her on the back patio. He hurried inside the guesthouse, swapped the towel for a pair of jeans and a t-shirt he left untucked and ran a hand through what was left of his hair, a good amount for a guy his age. Time to go in search of the high-heeled princess.

He knocked on the back door, hoping to catch her in the kitchen. If she was in any other part of the house, she most likely would not hear him. He was second-guessing his decision to return the wallet himself. She would have realized her mistake and returned to Murphy's by now. She didn't seem like a woman who didn't know where every penny was. Though he had a hand in her turning around and storming out of the tavern. He wanted her to smile at him once more instead of that death glare she gave him.

When she smiled, her features softened, like a cool breeze against the tall grass. When she locked up that grin tight, her face turned sour, and he suspected she could be every inch the rich bitch he thought she might be. He preferred the Claudia in flip-flops with her hair floating around her face and a smile that reached her eyes.

He walked around to the front, following the stone path on the east side of the house, and rang the bell. He didn't see any car in the driveway, but he couldn't remember if she had one. He had only seen her here and in town. She could walk to Main Street without any trouble. Maybe she didn't have a car. Or her driver was on vacation.

He tried the door. Locked. Best to get the key off his

key ring and let himself in through the back. He'd leave the wallet and a note. Or he'd just leave her wallet and let Sticks figure out for herself who was the kind neighbor. He doubted she would think it was him.

He followed the path through the garden of flowers. Vibrant colors in bloodreds, bright whites, true blues, and pinks like Claudia's shoes calmed him. Sweet smells filled the air, allowing him full-size breaths. He didn't permit himself too much pride, but he had created these beauties with time and patience. Growing them in many of the same ways he took care of the apple trees in his orchard. All because his mother had passed away, and her friend was missing her.

Hell, he still missed his mother and her ways, always having a smile for anyone who came to her door. Never raising her voice to her five boys, but rather using nothing except a stern look to corral them into behaving. Mom had been gone seven years already. Hard to believe. Growing those flowers was as much for him as it had been for Georgette as a way to keep his mother's memory close.

He had planted impatiens, roses, day lilies, and purple butterfly bushes among some annuals. He took care of creeping ground cover on the stone retaining walls, a few cherry blossom trees, and clary sage. Boxwoods stood guard for him in the places they were needed, filling in with their consistent green.

At night, strategically placed lighting accented the landscaping all year long. He was the one to replace those bulbs and set the timers. In the coldest months, he covered the bushes with bunting to protect them. This was his garden too. Claudia couldn't be allowed to sell this property to someone or something that would destroy what had been built over the years. He just wouldn't stand for that kind of destruction.

He went into the guest cottage to retrieve his keys. Even this place with its white walls and wood floors had a beauty to it. Staying here wasn't so bad. Fisting his keys, he returned for another journey back to the house.

"You have got to be kidding me." A voice drifted from the stone cottage up the slope. From his vantage point near the pool, he could only make out the point of the roof, but he didn't have to wonder who that was complaining up a storm.

He made a pivot and found Claudia standing in the doorway of the small stone cottage. "Everything okay?"

She jumped and squealed. Her gaze rested on him, and she clutched her chest. "Don't walk up to a woman like that. You scared me half to death."

"Apologies. I heard you yelling and came to investigate. Did you see a mouse or something?"

"Mouse? Where would a mouse fit in all of this?"

She pointed to the open door. Boxes, discarded furniture, and who knew what else stared back through the front door.

"When Carter said I had to clean out the stone cottage, he neglected to tell me it was filled floor to ceiling. Aunt Georgette was a hoarder." Claudia threw her hands into the air.

He tried to bite back the laugh but failed. She shot her death glare at him.

"Not exactly a true hoarder. But she did like to keep things from a bygone era."

"She kept things from every era. Probably all the way

79

back to the Revolutionary War. I can barely walk through there." Claudia wiped her hair out of her face. Her cheeks were flushed, and her eyes blazed. She still wore those fancy clothes she had on at Murphy's. Dirt streaked her white top, but what he liked was the way those black pants flattered her butt and stopped at her ankles.

Those impractical sticks were still on her feet too. A pink polish brightened her toes. He had missed that earlier. Nice toes. Before she caught him staring, he dragged his gaze back to her face.

"I guess you had better get started clearing things out then. Might want to change first. It's most likely dirty in there." He pointed to the spot on her shirt.

She swatted at the mess, but it did nothing to make it go away. He bit back the laugh ready to burst out. Her arms always seemed to windmill around when she spoke as if the story was out in front of her somehow.

"No need to gloat. You can save yourself the trouble. I'll have a dumpster here in a day. This town must have a few teenagers looking to make a buck."

"Ah. You can't hire help. Remember?" Had he actually given her a tip? If he had kept his mouth shut, she would have lost. That was what he wanted—wasn't it?

"Crap. I did forget. Okay, no teens. But I can get a dumpster and throw everything in it. There can't be anything worth saving in all that junk."

"Did you even look?" He wasn't sure about the value of the contents either, but he did know Georgette. She liked well-made things that lasted. And she didn't like to throw anything away that could be valuable someday.

And not stuff like old blankets or vintage clothing. Claudia could find a treasure in there.

"I can't get in there." She pointed at the door again, as if he hadn't seen it the first time. He tried not to laugh again.

"Might be something worth money. Something you could sell for cash." Cash was her king. She had practically said as much in Carter's office.

"Why did you come over here?" she said.

"I have this." He pulled her wallet out of his pocket. He had expected a woman like her would carry something bigger, made of fine leather, with a gold clasp. When Flora had said it was Claudia's, he almost didn't believe her. This wallet was small, fake leather with a snow scene on the front of it. Cute. Like her.

"You had it?" Her fingers slid over his when she grabbed for the wallet. He wanted to run his thumb over the inside of her hand to see if he could light up her eyes and find out if the warmth on his skin would travel further.

"I told Flora I would return it to you, seeing as we're roommates."

She pressed her lips into a thin line and glanced up at him through her lashes. "I wouldn't say that. But thank you. I went back to Murphy's and Flora had gone home for the day. No one there had seen the wallet, but the bartender was going to check with her. I almost canceled all the credit cards, but for some reason I came in here first. I actually couldn't stop myself. Stupid, but in the end it worked out. Weird, right?"

"Well, now you don't have to go to the trouble of

canceling anything." All those words floated in the air around him like soap bubbles. He wanted them to multiply until he was surrounded with the sound of her voice.

"Thank you," she said.

"It wasn't anything big. Just doing what any neighbor would do." He didn't want her thinking they were going to be friends now. He still planned on winning the competition no matter how pretty he thought she was.

Her smile struggled to stay on her face and he wondered what he could do to keep it there. "Where I'm from I don't even know my neighbors. I can't imagine anyone finding my wallet and bringing it to me."

"Doesn't sound very welcoming."

"I guess not." She held up the wallet. "Thank you again."

"Don't think twice about it. I'll be seeing you." He needed to get the hell out of there and turned to go. She made him think about things he didn't usually pay much attention to.

And he wanted to see more of her legs than just those ankles. And he wanted to make her laugh. He couldn't figure that one out at all. She was nothing but snobby and ornery around him, yet she intrigued him in some strange way. Maybe because he saw glimpses of who she might actually be if they met under other circumstances.

"Silas?"

He turned back to her. "Yes?"

"Would you like to have a glass of wine with me? It's been a tough day, and I don't like to drink alone." Her hands fidgeted with the wallet, but her gaze stayed locked on his.

"I'm not much of a wine man." Spending time with her would cost him. He couldn't let his guard down for the next three weeks. He needed to save the mansion and his garden.

"Sure. I get it. We're sworn enemies. I'm sure you have plans with your family or something anyway." She waved her hand through the air as if to erase what she had said. Her smile wilted.

"If you give me a little while, I'll grab some beer and come back."

He wanted to kick himself, but he was always a sucker for a woman in distress. That sad look on her face clamped his mouth shut around his objections.

Her face lit up, pushing the discontent away like a good pair of windshield wipers. "Great. I'll see you on the patio in an hour."

"See you then."

One drink wouldn't hurt. It didn't have to change anything between them at all.

CHAPTER SEVEN

Claudia ran through the kitchen, putting dishes in the dishwasher and trying to find a beer glass that didn't have a crack in it. Georgette had plenty of glasses, but for some reason many of them were damaged. She didn't want to think about the glasses being a metaphor for herself. Not with Silas coming back for a drink. When the dumpster arrived, all the broken pieces of Georgette's existence would find their way to it. And maybe a few pieces of hers as well.

Asking Silas to stay for a drink had rushed from her mouth before she even realized she had said it. She couldn't bear the idea of facing that awful cottage filled with who knew what, and she had no desire to face a long evening inside this oversized money pit.

Silas had looked so good in his simple t-shirt and jeans. The edge of his hair was still wet from a recent shower, and she wondered if he had used the outdoor one again. Her mind conjured images of him in that towel. She had wanted to spend time with him, damn it.

Getting too close to him was stupid. They could never be friends. He didn't even like her. And he was so far removed from her real life, he would never fit in there. They were competitors. Had he agreed to have a drink with her so he could get to know her better and use that against her somehow? Well, two could play at that game—assuming that game was on.

But first, she needed to wipe the counters and take a peek at the bathroom. The construction crew had used the half bath off the kitchen. She hadn't wanted to look in there for fear of what she would find. Armed with disinfectant spray, she peered around the door.

"Well, it's not as if he has far to go home if he needs a bathroom." She shot spray into the room and closed the door. Another day's project.

She didn't have any picky food either. It wasn't as if this was a date. She didn't need to feed the man. A simple glass of wine for her and a beer for him. After that, she could send him on his way.

When he had appeared, and her heart rate had returned to normal, those blue eyes of his had turned on a flame inside her. For a minute, she had forgotten that she didn't like him and that he was the one person keeping her from her future. She only wanted to sit with him because his self-assured quiet demeanor brought a sense of peace around her that she rarely felt.

He carried himself with a collectedness that oozed off him. She gathered that most things worked out well for him—a big family, children, a successful business, a town that liked and probably admired him. She hadn't missed the way Flora smiled when he materialized at her side. The familiarness Silas and Flora seemed to share had made her a little jealous, if she were being honest.

Time ticked past the hour he said he would return by, and the sun dipped a little lower, hanging between the tree branches. She shouldn't be surprised. He wasn't coming back. She put the glasses away and slid out of heels. Her feet were killing her. Walking on the stone floor in the kitchen didn't help any.

She popped a frozen pizza in the oven. Not much of a dinner, and one she would most likely regret five minutes after she ate it, but it was easy and that's what she needed at the moment.

She also needed to put her feet up and forget about the day. Where that would be, other than her bedroom, she had no clue.

Ladders in varying heights and degree of filth filled the foyer like an obstacle course. Area rugs were rolled up and pushed to the side. Buckets of plasters and paint filled the living room. Electric wires spun out from wall sockets. A dining table with swirls carved into its edge and large enough to accommodate twelve occupied most of the dining room. The ornate chairs, though lovely, were covered in dust and in serious need of an uphol-sterer. Chaos and clutter made her twitch.

Other furniture had been relocated to the dining room—extra chairs, a sideboard, and two random end tables. None of the rooms in the front of the house were comfortable enough to cuddle in with a good book.

She ran upstairs to Georgette's old bedroom—the one she was using now—and changed into a pair of thin sweatpants and a tank top. She had about twenty minutes before the pizza was done. Plenty of time to move a few things downstairs and create a spot for her to unwind at night.

Opposite the kitchen was a small room with low ceilings and fantastic wood beams that needed a good coat of stain. A small fireplace took up one corner by the window. The fireplace might have been original to the house. A selling feature, if the thing actually worked. She would need Van to take a look at that and fix it if it didn't. She also loved the built-in shelf under the window where Georgette kept a few classic books. Jane Austen. Charles Dickens. Truman Capote. A layer of dust covered each book much like the dining room furniture.

Aunt Georgette may have held a garden party every year, but did she ever have guests over to spend time with? Had she ever enjoyed these books? From what Claudia knew of the woman, she didn't think Georgette had enjoyed much of anything.

This adorable room was empty of any furniture, and she couldn't figure out why. Sure, the floors needed sanding and some of the boards might need to be replaced, but the room for the most part was usable. Maybe the contractors had plans to set up a break room or something in there. Van had mentioned not wanting to use the kitchen and bother her since he was here a lot.

Well, she would claim this small space for a little rest and relaxation. Van would have to settle for the kitchen. She opened one of the windows to let in some air. The room faced the side yard. Not the spectacular view from the kitchen windows that faced the garden and the pool, but this room offered intimacy and warmth. Something she lacked in her life.

She dragged a small camelback sofa with cream-colored material from the dining room into the den. That's what she would call the room in the house listing when the time came. Getting the sofa free required moving some of the dining chairs as it was wedged between the wall and the chairs.

She arranged the sofa against the far wall, facing the fireplace in case it worked. Then she retrieved a wood end table with a marble top and a lamp tucked into the corner of the dining room beside the cabinet. She still didn't understand why so much furniture had been shoved into one room when the house had plenty of space. This home really could work as a small boutique hotel. Plenty of bedrooms upstairs, most of which had their own baths. Downstairs boasted several rooms for guests to lounge and wander between. Even the foyer, once void of the ladders, would make a good reception area.

By the time she was done yanking, tugging, and dragging, she had worked up a good sweat and swept her hair up onto the top of her head.

The pizza was slightly overcooked, but she was proud of her little accomplishment. In fact, she would take the food and the wine and sit in there with one of Georgette's neglected books.

A knock on the back door startled her. Silas, looking toward the flowers, waited with a bag in his hand. She hesitated. He hadn't seen her yet. She should leave him out there, thinking she had either gone out or gone to bed and wanted nothing to do with him.

But maybe he had a good excuse for running late. They hadn't exchanged numbers. He wouldn't have been able to call her. She caved and opened the door.

"Hi," he said with a full-wattage smile. She refused to fall prey to its charm. She should tell him to take his bag and go. If he couldn't have the decency to return in a timely manner, he would probably never take her feelings into account.

"I didn't think you were coming any longer." She remained in the doorway to prove a point. One she wasn't sure he understood, but it made her feel better to refuse his entry for a beat or two. Because she highly doubted she would send him away. She craved company.

"I'm sorry I'm later than I said. I should've called you. Nice feet, Sticks. You should walk around barefoot more often." He pointed at her bare toes.

A devilish grin spread across his face and heat flamed her cheeks. She shouldn't enjoy the fact he noticed her feet so often. And now he went and made it impossible to send him away.

"Well, come in. I made a pizza for myself. It's getting cold, and I want to enjoy it." She left him at the door and went back to the stove where the pizza waited on a cookie sheet. Thankfully, the pizza was already cut because she had no idea if a pizza cutter even existed in this ancient kitchen.

"Do you feel like sharing some?" He followed her in and placed a Wilde Orchard bag on the table.

"Not with someone who's late when they're invited over for a drink." She tossed the snide remark over her shoulder to see what he would do with it.

"Not even after that great compliment?" He arched a brow.

"Nope." She might be flirting with this man, and she needed to stop that immediately. This was not a date.

This was just her doing something dumb and asking him to have a drink with her. Damn her loneliness.

"I really had meant to come straight back. While I was out getting beer, I made a quick stop at the orchard. I grabbed an apple pie, and then my son needed me for a few things that couldn't wait. It's our busy season. I'm sorry."

"Thank you." She fought the disappointment in her voice. He owed her nothing. They weren't even friends.

"I don't have your number. Or I would have called. I guess I could've called Carter to get it, but honestly, I didn't think about it. I know that sounds bad, but it's not personal. Not this time anyway." He barked out a laugh.

She had to give him credit for his honesty. They were on rocky ground at best, and he had brought over her wallet. He was a decent guy even if he was stuck in the past and couldn't appreciate progress and how any hotel chain would do wonders with this place.

"Give me your cell. I'll put it in." She held out her hand, but he didn't budge.

"I don't have a cell."

"Who doesn't have a cell phone?" He didn't need to lie on her account. And here she was thinking he was so honest.

"Well, I don't have the kind everyone has today with all the apps."

"Seriously? You still have a flip phone?"

"Cross my heart." He mimed the gesture and looked adorable doing it. "Except it was destroyed when the tree fell on my house."

"A tree fell on your house? That's why you're living

in Georgette's guest cottage? Were you in the house when it happened?"

"I happened to be out. I got lucky. The phone didn't. And I don't know if I'll replace it."

"Why not? Are you against phones or something?"

"Something. Are you ready to share that pizza?"

She had yet to meet anyone who didn't have a smartphone. Even her coworker Miriam who was eighty and worked at the hotel's dry cleaner had a smartphone. She loved showing everyone pictures of her grandkids.

"I suppose." She tore away a slice and put it on a plate for him. She added napkins and a fork just in case he cut his food, and a glass for the beer which he ignored, opening the bottle and taking a swig.

They sat at the table as the shadows grew longer and spread their darkness in the corners outside. She didn't know this man, but he knew Georgette and what she was like. It would be nice to learn a few things about the woman who may change her life and her motivations behind it.

"You must've known Georgette pretty well for her to leave you half her estate." She picked at the pizza. The gooey cheese had hardened some and the sauce was too sweet. But the wine was good.

He wiped his hands on a napkin. "I knew her my entire life."

"You're kidding?" She had never known an adult from her childhood to now. She and her mother had moved around a lot. Building long-term relationships with anyone had been difficult.

So many times she had longed for a mentor-type person to lean on. Her mother had few friends while she was alive. Georgette and her sister, Claudia's maternal grandmother, were never the kind of close sisters depicted on television, so she hardly knew her aunt.

"Georgette being a part of my life surprises you?" Silas put another slice of pizza on each of their plates.

"I guess it does." She shouldn't be shocked having spent a little time in this small town and yet she was because Georgette never seemed like she wanted anyone around all that much.

"Georgette and my mother were best friends. She spent a lot of time at our house. She said she preferred the chaos at our place over the quiet tomb she referred to her house as."

"What kind of chaos?" Another shocker. Georgette with her stuffy personality didn't seem like the kind of person who'd be drawn to a house full of noise and commotion.

"It was always loud with five boys and my parents. We played rough. Our friends were always in and out. We lived on the orchard so our employees were always coming and going too. I think Georgette enjoyed having us all around her."

She could imagine Silas as a younger man with a head full of wavy hair and fewer lines on his textured skin. He leaned into his age nicely, better than a lot of men, but she could imagine a lanky Silas with sinewy muscles and that slow walk the girls would mistake for the arrogant swagger of a teenager.

"Sounds nice." She had grown up with her mom. She loved her mom very much, but her mother was always working hard to make ends meet. Two jobs often. They usually lived in a one-bedroom apartment. Sometimes a two-bedroom if they were lucky. But they moved a lot because Mom was always looking for cheaper rent or because the latest slumlord made their living arrangements unbearable.

"Like any family, we had our good times and our bad. What about you? Did you grow up in a big house like this one? Summered at the shore? Maybe sleep away camp as a kid? Had a high school friend named Biffy." His smile touched his eyes. He was joking, but she didn't want to correct him. She would spare him the stories of growing up without. He wouldn't be able to relate, having the support of a large family to cushion the blow when life swung hard.

"No friend named Biffy." That was as much truth as she would reveal.

Her summers were spent working at whatever hotel her mother did. She had started in housekeeping and learned as much as she could. She had learned it was important to make friends with the right people—not just the management and never the hotel guests. To the guests she was invisible just like her mother always was. She had hated that.

She had become friends with the kitchen staff. The security department. The concierge. The guys in valet. She asked questions and gathered information so that by the time she went to college, community first for two years, she had more experience than any other student in her hotel management program.

Rising to the top took some time and many hard knocks, but she had made it. And she wasn't ashamed to say, though never to Silas Wilde who sat opposite her in his blue t-shirt that brought out his eyes even more, that

the one time she had married was for money. She had
cared for him, but not the right way. When she had realized her mistake, she had left—without a cent.

"You aren't eating your pizza," he said, snapping her
out of her reverie.

"It's overcooked." She wasn't hungry anymore and
the wine turned sour on her tongue.

"Then it's time for apple pie." He slid out of the seat
and plucked a white pie box out of the bag.

The box had the Wilde Orchard logo on it too.
Suddenly, she didn't know what she was doing in that
kitchen having dinner and dessert with the man who had
the power to uproot her from her plans. He wasn't going
to stick around and make sure she landed on her feet no
matter how cute he might think they are. She had only
herself to rely on and couldn't risk the security of her
golden years.

She and Silas should not be forging friendships. They
were adversaries, and she had best remember that or she
would find herself not just alone, but alone and broke.
Not a good look.

He reached for the drawer with the silverware and
went straight to the cabinet with the dishes. He knew his
way around this house. Of course, he did. He had probably spent most of his life in this kitchen that had gone
from in style to vintage over the decades.

He knew this town too. He fit in here. The place
belonged to him. She fit in nowhere. No one was waiting
for her. And a piece of apple pie and a handsome man
weren't going to change that.

"I'm sorry, Silas. But I think the wine gave me a

headache. Can I take a rain check on the pie?" She grabbed their plates and dumped them in the sink.

He regarded her. His eyebrows narrowed briefly, but then snapped straight. "Sure. No problem." He put the pie back in the bag but didn't move to take it.

She went to the door and opened it, leaving no question that the evening was over. The sun had almost disappeared, but the humidity stayed. The vibrant colors of the day had wrung out, but the landscape lighting had popped on, leaving small globes of warm light in a pattern along the walkway. It was lovely. Warm and welcoming without pretense. Just like him.

"Thanks for the pizza." He shoved his hands in his jeans pockets.

"You're not taking the pie or the beer."

"You keep them. I'll see you around, Claudia." Her name came out like softened butter on freshly baked bread.

"See you." She closed the door behind him but watched as he followed the path back to the guest cottage.

He took his time, stopping once to adjust the lighting. He rubbed his fingers over some of the petals. He was deliberate and considerate. She couldn't help but wonder why a man like him had no wife. He was the whole package. And terrible for her.

CHAPTER EIGHT

Silas hesitated outside Brad's office. Brad was on the phone. The call sounded personal, and Silas didn't want to interrupt. He was also stalling because once he asked his question, Brad would have a few of his own that Silas wasn't prepared to answer.

Brad ended the call. He couldn't go on standing in the hallway. Someone would come along and wonder what he was doing.

Silas knocked on the open door. "Hey, son."

"Hey, Dad. What's up?" Brad put his phone on the desk.

Brad's office was unlike most vice president offices. His was filled with the remnants of a farmer's life. A stack of small apple crates went up one wall. He had one metal filing cabinet with pictures of his daughter Winter on top and magazines about agriculture. More pictures of Winter were on his desk with small tools to perform a quick fix on equipment.

Brad also displayed pictures Winter had drawn and

taped them to the walls. Brad didn't look like most vice presidents either with his hair to his shoulders, but Silas detected it was a little shorter than last time he saw his son. And then there were the tattoos all over his wide arms. None of that mattered to Silas. Brad was everything he could want in a son. Even when he had been a roaring pain in Silas' ass. He never wanted to repeat the teen years, especially with having twins. Brad and Brooklyn had tested his very last nerve on some occasions.

"I was wondering if I could use your computer for a little while today?" He leaned against the wall, careful not to wrinkle one of his granddaughter's masterpieces.

"You want to use the computer? Why?" Brad straightened a pile of papers, glancing from the desk back to him.

"Research." He held up the thick folder with all of Georgette's notes.

"What is that mess?" Here came the questions.

"Something I can't get heads nor tails out of." Searching through Georgette's thick folder had proven unhelpful. She had a filing system that he guessed only she could understand. Receipts and order forms were in no order. Something from thirty years ago had been on the top while a list of food choices from last year's event had been shoved in the middle of the pack. He had nearly set the whole damn thing on fire when he realized he was no better off than a blind man alone in a dark tunnel.

"Are you doing some kind of data entry?" Brad narrowed his eyes.

"I need to start planning the garden party. I thought

the computer might be faster to look up some information."

He could hunt and peck his way around a computer, but he didn't like it, and he didn't own one. Phone books were a thing of the past, and he needed to gather information on a couple of the vendors he thought Georgette had used. He also didn't have the time to go to the library where he still visited when he wanted to learn a thing or two about the world he lived in.

"This party again. Dad, Georgette was out of her mind. I'm sorry. You know I liked her. She was always good to Grandma, but I think she lost it at the end, giving you a party to plan and setting up that competition between you and her *never seen before* niece."

"I'm not that helpless." Normally, he never minded when the kids or his brothers ribbed him about his life choices. He liked his life and wouldn't apologize for it. He had raised his children in that cabin that may have been small and without luxuries, but they both turned out fine. And loved him despite their strange upbringing.

But lately, the implications that he couldn't take care of himself or handle a task that required technology grated on him. He could learn what he didn't know, and he knew more than he let on. His family could use a dose of *I'll show you*.

"Let Lyra help you." Brad pushed out of his chair and came around the desk.

Every time he stood beside his son and looked him straight in the eye, he could not fathom where the years went and that not only was his son his height—not entirely a shock—but that Brad was a man almost forty with a daughter and two soon to be stepsons.

"I can handle it. And I'm not supposed to have help. Georgette's stipulations." And even if he could have the help and not lose the competition, Lyra was busy enough running two businesses and raising three kids with Brad.

"No one has to know, Dad. Lyra and I aren't going to tell. And from what you mentioned about this Claudia Jacobs, she's only going to turn the house over to the highest bidder if she wins. Candlewood Falls doesn't need a conglomerate coming in and messing with the structure of this town. It could cause trouble for the orchard down the road."

"I won't lie. I'll win fair and square."

"Were you always this stubborn, or is this a new thing?" Brad laughed and patted him on the shoulder, knowing the answer to his question.

"Depends on who you ask." His ex-wife, Brad and Brooklyn's mother, would say he was as stubborn as the day was long. His brothers might say the very same thing. He wondered what Claudia thought of him, but he forced the thought away.

Sitting in her kitchen the other night, sharing food and drink, was the easiest it had been in a long time to talk with a woman. She had been adorable with her hair piled on top of her head and wearing those thin gray sweatpants that outlined her firm butt and trim legs. The bare feet had been a bonus. She had seemed so at ease — relaxed even — at first.

He hadn't expected to like her at all, but he did. He liked the way she listened as if everything he said was important, or the way she scrunched up her nose when she laughed. He really liked the way she would tuck her foot under her while she picked at her pizza.

"Don't let the computer fall asleep. You need my fingerprint to start it back up," Brad said, interrupting his pleasant thoughts of Claudia's thin ankles.

"Doesn't it have some kind of password?" He knew that much about those machines.

"Not this one. Just my print."

"Will you be on the property somewhere?" They owned a hundred acres that included the apple trees, a bed and breakfast, and the farmhouse where he and his brothers grew up along with several buildings for the apples.

"I'm heading out for the day. Winter is having some kind of field day at school for the end of the year, and I've been ordered to attend."

"I never imagined you as such a softie, going to school events or letting half your house be decorated in pink. That girl has you wrapped around all her fingers."

"Yeah, me either, especially the pink stuff. I swear it looks like bubble gum threw up all over the place. But I'm not the only one, Grandpa." Brad pointed at him with a sideways glance.

"Guilty as charged."

"If you get stuck on the computer, I think Sam is around. Give him a holler. He'll come and help." Brad headed for the door.

"Got it." He didn't need Sam's help. He had used Google before. He just didn't like the idea everything he searched was kept somewhere and used. His life was his own, and he wanted real privacy. Not the pretend privacy others believed they had.

"Oh," Brad said, turning back. "Dad, did you lose your cell phone in the cabin accident? Brooklyn said she's been trying to reach you, but you haven't called back."

"Is she okay?"

"She's fine. She was checking on you. I think she's worried you're the one who isn't okay."

"I'll call her while I'm here." He could make a stop by her place too and spend a little time with his grandbaby and those alpacas. The alpacas were always good to put a smile on his face. Goofy creatures.

"Does this mean you won't get a second phone?"

"I might. I'm not in a rush. Have too many other important things to take care of." He waved the over-sized folder.

"If you don't replace it, I'm going to tell Winter you don't want a phone anymore."

Winter had been trying her darndest to convince him to get a phone with a screen and all those apps. She wanted to send him a picture every day so he could send one back to her. She had called it a snap or snapped. Like his mind would be if he had to use a phone like that.

He had put her off by saying he already had a phone and it wasn't practical to change it until it stopped working. She had bought his excuse, but it was no longer true.

"That's devilish, Bradford."

"What was it you just said? Guilty as charged." Brad winked and hurried out of the office.

His children and his grandchildren knew how to play him and that included Lyra's boys. When one of them wanted to go fishing, all it took was a quick call. He stopped. *A call.* Brooklyn had tried to call him. His granddaughter wanted to reach him.

Okay, they won. He'd get a new phone. Maybe Huck

would go with him and help him pick one. He could also use the excuse he would need a way for these vendors to reach him for the party.

Georgette was probably having a good laugh from her spot in the hereafter. She had always tried to get him to return to his old ways of life, thinking he was out of his mind to cut off civilization so much. He hadn't known how effective grandchildren could be.

He sat behind Brad's desk and opened the search engine. He had brought a clean notebook of his own for this little event. On the first page he had listed some of the caterers he thought Georgette might have used, but he had no phone numbers for or the numbers had worn away over the years and he couldn't make them out.

He searched, but being hunched over the computer didn't accomplish much besides putting a crick in his neck and tightening his shoulders into knots that might never come loose. After an hour, he had called only two places and left messages. Not a lot accomplished this afternoon.

He would have to resume this activity later. Which could mean a trip to the library after all, or a stop at someone's house to use their computer. Brooklyn would let him use hers.

Food needed to be secured along with chairs and tables. He only knew about those because of a sticky note Georgette had attached to a picture of the tables dressed in their linens. Flowers he could handle. He had helped her in years past cut flowers from her garden for vases on the tables. Where were the vases? If they were somewhere in the big house, Claudia might try to keep them from him.

His back cracked as he pushed from the chair. He would take a final pass through the fields to see how the men were doing and if the cold room's thermostat was acting up again, then he'd stop at Brooklyn's before grabbing an early dinner and forging ahead with his plans for the party.

He truly didn't know what he was doing and was in way over his head. He should take Lyra up on her offer to help him and keep it a secret. What harm would it really cause and who would know?

He would, and he wanted to be able to look Claudia in the eye. Even if he lost, he would do it with his dignity intact. Playing fair was the only way to play. He would never tolerate a cheat and any competitor who used underhanded measures to win was the lowest of the low.

Disappointment curled around his gut and gave a squeeze as he packed up the folder and headed outside, passing customers in the flower garden on the orchard where they could cut flowers for themselves and take them home. Apples wouldn't be ready for picking for a couple of months.

He had wanted to check a few things off his list today, but no luck. Planning this party proved harder than he had first believed.

"Silas, wait up."

He turned to see Huck hurrying toward him. "Are you working today?"

"Was just about to take a loop around the fields. Those trees in the west corner were showing some bug problems. We tried a new solution to stop the spread before we lost the whole variety. Do you need something?"

"Nah. I'm good. How's the party planning coming?" Huck barked out a laugh.

"Not funny. Except I have barely begun. I'm spinning my wheels right now."

"Why don't you just buy the house yourself and forget about this whole thing? That lady in the big house doesn't want to hang around here, and you sure as hell can afford to buy it."

"What am I going to do with a house that size?"

"Live in it."

"I don't want a house big enough for ten families or all its extra buildings. I want to live in my cabin." Which he still couldn't do and didn't know when he would be able to either. The tree was still lying across it because all the local landscapers were busy this time of year and extra busy from that storm that tore down that tree. Plenty of other trees went down too. No one could put him on the schedule.

"You are a stubborn fool," Huck said.

Yeah, stubborn was the word his family would use to describe him. Maybe he was, but he liked the way he was. He wasn't bothering anyone with his way of life. He didn't do any damage.

"Maybe. But it's my life. I never asked you to change when you were running around causing all kinds of ruckus with that group of ignorant men you were hanging with. And you had far more reasons to make a switch. You could've hurt someone. And that group nearly destroyed Caleb."

"True enough. I have a lot to make amends for, and I'm working on it. I'm not perfect and never will be. I lost my way, but I'm coming back. Doesn't mean I don't see what's happening to you."

"What's that?"

"You're getting tired of that way of life you've been so committed to. You can deny it all you want, but remember it was me you shared a room with growing up. Ten years ago, you would've dragged that tree off your house with your bare hands if you had to. Now, you're accepting the excuse that there isn't a landscaper in this county with time on their hands for you. No one is going to judge you for making a change. Not your kids and not me. You can put down your pride now and come back to the way of the living."

"I don't know what you're talking about." Pride had not been the reason he had moved up the mountain.

The world had changed back then, and he didn't like where he saw things going. He had married a woman driven by possessions, making him crazy with all the things she had wanted. Every time he had come home, something new and expensive waited for him to see.

He had needed to pull the plug, to check out for a while. He hadn't fit in the world, disagreeing with the politics, the fast pace, and the pursuit of items. If he hadn't lived in Candlewood Falls where he knew everyone, he would've found a place just like it. Living here with its simple ways, where everyone looked out for each other, was how he could stay in the living as Huck had put it.

"I think you know exactly what I'm talking about. You had a point to prove once. I understand that. I did too. Maybe being sandwiched in between our brothers made us want to stretch out and find something that belonged to only us. You with the cabin and me with the Brotherhood of Watchman. But it's time to give it up."

"Huck, enough. I've got plenty on my plate without having to put up with your opinions. I'm just fine the way I am." He wouldn't think about enjoying the guesthouse at all, or sitting at the table with Claudia talking over a meal. He didn't even care that meal tasted like cardboard. It had been a long time since he had enjoyed a woman's company.

For the briefest of seconds, he wanted to taste life the way other people had it. And then that desire was gone. Because the beautiful woman had thrown him out.

CHAPTER NINE

C laudia dumped the lasagna in the trash. That was the second batch she had burned because the oven's temperature was off. It might also have to do with the fact that thing stepped out of the nineteen fifties and never left. Or she simply stunk at all things culinary. She never cooked for herself. Living in a hotel most of her life meant a kitchen filled with other people creating artistic meals at her disposal. And when that wasn't an option, she could walk to the corner and grab something quick. But that was not the case in this town. She was still adjusting to the fact many of the stores on Main Street closed early.

Now that her car had arrived earlier today from Chicago, she may have to venture outside the town limits to find a late-night restaurant.

She had promised two meals to Eudora by the end of the day and had completed nothing. Without more time, she would have to buy a tray from somewhere, making her look like someone who didn't care about others enough to bother. Even if she didn't plan on staying in this town, that didn't mean she was heartless. A woman needed help. The least she could do was lend a hand.

She needed to get the food to Eudora, then come back and tackle some of that cottage. Silas probably had the whole party planned by now. There wasn't a person in this town or most likely any of the neighboring towns who would tell the man no.

Sleep had evaded her last night, making her impatient all day with the contractors and the cooking. Some creature with lots of legs and long nails had run back and forth across the attic floor above her bedroom all night. She had spent half the night sitting up in bed with the covers pulled up to her neck, watching the ceiling. Whatever kind of night animal it was, scurried around the attic as if to taunt her and to let her know whose house it really was.

She had sent the contractors up there this morning when the crew arrived, but they said they couldn't find anything. They must've lied. What if it was a bat? The idea of a bat made her shiver. She hated bats.

"Hi, Claudia," Van said, sticking his head in the kitchen and wrinkling his nose. "Something smells like it was burned."

"Yeah. My multiple failed attempts to cook."

"Do you need some help?" He stepped into the room, wearing a Hunter's Construction t-shirt and cargo shorts. A tool belt was strung around his waist. She could see the Wilde family resemblance in his face, and she wondered what Silas had been like as a young man. Probably the same grouchy guy, just with less gray in his hair.

"No, thanks." She couldn't let it get around town that her cooking skills were lacking, but she needed her contractor to help her make lasagna. And with Van being related to Silas, her competitor would have knowledge of her ineptitude in minutes. She understood the small-town telephone line game. She shouldn't care that Silas would find out about her inabilities, but she did. He was probably an incredible cook.

"What I need is an oven from this decade."

"I'll let Dean know."

She couldn't let Silas get ahead of her even if she still felt guilty for throwing him out the other night. She liked him. That was the problem, plain and simple. She couldn't afford to fall for a man like him—someone ingrained in his town and who judged her for having money.

"Let's renovate the kitchen last." It was hard enough having men in and out, fixing this and changing that. Having them under foot in the heart of a house, would drive her mad.

"No problem. I'm going to work on demoing the upstairs bathrooms. Dean told me which two needed updates. This place is going to look amazing when we're done. Are you planning on staying here?"

"Why does everyone think I need to stick around? I hardly knew my aunt. I didn't want this house. Now I have a headache a mile long to contend with because she willed half of it to me." Her words snapped and cut, if Van's shocked expression and visible backing up were any indication.

"I'm sorry," she said. "I'm not myself. No sleep." And she just didn't bounce back as easily without sleep any longer. Some days she missed the energy she had twenty years ago. Her frustration also mounted at the level of work required of the stone cottage.

"Hey, I get it. You're taking on a lot with the renos and some of the problems we've had. The whole town has heard about your competition with my uncle. That can't be easy either." He shoved his hands in his pockets.

"It's not a big deal. I'll handle it." She always did. She had only herself to rely on most of her life. Why should now be any different?

"I'm sure you will. Well, I'd better get to work. I'm behind schedule. Dean wanted the floor ripped up in that blue bathroom a week ago."

"I want those renovations done as soon as possible. Dean knows that."

"He sure does and so do I. I won't let you down." He turned to go.

"Hang on a second. Do you know a good Italian place that can whip up a decent lasagna quickly?" She would have to admit defeat and order in. She didn't have time to try again or fight with the Ultramatic Caloric range.

Van gave her the name of a place in Clinton. She pulled up their website, placed the order, and waited. They had said an hour. She could go out to the cottage and begin to clean it out, but she didn't want to get started and have to stop. After she dropped off the food to Eudora, she would have a quick bite and then begin. She should have a couple of hours of daylight still. Hopefully, the cottage had electricity. Then she could set up some lights and keep going.

She pulled out the open bottle of wine from her night

with Silas and poured a little, taking it into the den. She needed to stop thinking about him and looking for him on the property. Her luck had failed her today each time she sought a glimpse of him in the outdoor shower. No gander of his bare chest or a towel wrapped around his waist.

He was an eccentric man. She wanted to know more about him, but she didn't dare. She had learned enough. Her only mission in this town should be to win and go. Romance was for other women.

Talbot sent her a text about a possible interview for her in New York at a major hotel next week. Her insides sparked with excitement, but fizzled out right away. Did she really want to start over in a new city? But where would she go? She couldn't stay here even if she wanted to. She needed to sell her half of the house to have money to live on if she didn't have a job. Her little savings would only go so far.

Whether she liked it or not, no one knocked on her proverbial door, asking her to come work for them. What she had done to defend Louisa would be everywhere in the industry like a bad virus. Instead of applauding her for standing up against harassment, her colleagues shunned her. She should jump at the chance to interview. *Interview*. After all her years running The Barry Watson, she had been demoted to interviewing.

She gulped down some wine. Chicago was her city of choice, but she couldn't afford to be picky. Especially if she lost to Silas which seemed unthinkable, but she had to be a realist. He had advantages over her.

Once the competition was over, she might be without a place to live. If Silas won, he would throw her out, and she had her pride. Her bags would be packed right away.

She sent a text back to Talbot to set it up. It wouldn't hurt to see what they offered. She was missing the hustle and bustle of a city, but she had to admit, it was so nice to sit outside at night with the warm air around her and hear nothing but the cicadas and her own breathing. Or occasionally the pool filter.

Candlewood Falls wasn't all bad. Everyone that was from here seemed to love it. But she wasn't from here. And she never would be. Small towns didn't often welcome strangers. But a stranger attached to Silas Wilde might get some leeway. Who was she kidding? Silas was not interested in her at all. He was just a kind man with a sarcastic streak for her.

Her eyelids grew heavy as she sipped the wine. The room was cozy, and the book was lulling her. Damn whatever had been in the attic last night causing a commotion and scaring her half to death. She had been partly tempted to run and get Silas, but she figured he would laugh at her, the city girl who couldn't live in the country. So she had stayed awake all night watching for signs of the ceiling falling in on her and some oversized rodent with pointy teeth coming after her.

She would rest her eyes for just a minute. The food wouldn't be ready for a while. She stretched out her legs and closed her eyes.

Jumping with a start, Claudia forced her vision to focus. Darkness covered the room in thick layers. Her brain took a minute to catch up to the space around her. She had been resting her eyes just a minute ago. Had she slept through the night? She fumbled for her phone. Not the whole night, but it was nine o'clock.

"Nine?" she said and ran for the kitchen. She had never picked up the food. Eudora was waiting.

She grabbed her keys and hurried out the door, not even bothering to see if Van was still in the house. He could let himself out or might have already. Something was always taking his attention away from this project.

The streets of Candlewood Falls were mostly dark once she got off Main Street. Traffic lights and sidewalks were absent from these foreign roads, forcing her to drive in the center of the lane, clutching the steering wheel with both hands, avoiding where the road dipped into the grass. She couldn't see beyond her high beams and would never get used to driving around here.

Her GPS directed her to the restaurant that was in a small strip of stores on a main road. The building didn't look like much with its flat roof and stucco side. It sat almost on the street with very little space for the parking spots out front, but Van had insisted it was the best Italian food around.

With her food secured in the back, she inputted Eudora's address and hit the road again. Everything in this town was stretched out like a bouncing putty pulled to its extreme. She didn't even know New Jersey had this much open space. She thought the whole state looked like the area surrounding the airport with its oil refineries and industrial complexes polluting the air. Fooled her. And it was a nice surprise, actually.

She pulled into a long drive. At least she hoped it was the correct driveway. All the mailboxes were on one side of the road, and it wasn't this one. The left side of the road was completely dark with no lights of any kind. If she had to guess, a farm or a park or the black abyss rolled along that side. On the other side, most of the houses sat far back off the road. They offered nothing in the way of light.

On faith and assurance from Our Lady GPS, she took the driveway and parked by the three-car garage. The house yawned into the night sky. A second-story chandelier was lit and visible from the extra-wide window, showcasing it. A few other windows on the first and second floors glowed warm with gold light too. A porched wrapped around one side. The regal wood double front doors with etched glass gave her pause. The home was welcoming and untouchable at the same time.

She pushed out of the car, wondering what Eudora did for a living that she could afford such a vast house by herself. Did she too have a relative who left her money? Her relative probably didn't include a monkey-chase to obtain it like crazy Aunt Georgette had.

A chill had kicked up, cooling the humid air. A storm was scheduled for overnight. Long after she should be home. A good thing since she didn't want to be on these dark roads while it was raining hard. A flash of lightning cut through the sky in the distance. She wished she had not fallen asleep and delivered this food hours ago, mostly because she had failed Eudora, but also because she didn't relish the twist and turns of the Candlewood Falls roads during a storm.

The two trays weighed her arms down. She had to juggle them to close the trunk and gingerly made her way to the door. Her high heels may have been a bad choice out here in the middle of what she would now refer to as Camp Crystal Lake country. Anyone could be lurking in the substantial darkness that swallowed up everything around her, claiming it for itself. She craved a little white noise and a traffic jam right now.

She rang the bell and waited. Her heart ached with how she had let this woman down. She had wanted to help, and she had botched it up completely. Eudora would probably tell everyone in her inner circle and before the sun had a chance to brighten the day, Silas would get wind of her mistake.

She had wanted to prove to Silas that she wasn't all about the money without having to say it. A kind gesture would allow him to see that she understood hardship and was a team player. Or was she trying to prove that to herself? Had she forgotten where she came from, lately? Standing up for Louisa had been a harsh reminder and that was why she had reacted so vehemently, taking the steak knife from Louisa and poking the point in that man's neck.

She would not allow anyone to use their power, physical or otherwise, to harass a weaker person. When she had walked into that hotel room, seeing red was an understatement. The desire to show that man he had no right to anything that wasn't his had consumed her.

Minutes ticked by. Either Eudora wasn't home or wasn't coming to the door. And Claudia was done with standing on the porch, trying to see into the shadows. She'd leave the food by the door and send a text, stating as such.

The door swung open, spilling light at her feet. A tall woman with dark eyes and light-brown skin pressed her lips together in a slight smile. She wore a pretty beige floral top and shorts that hung loose on her. Her cheeks were gaunt and her eyes hooded.

"Can I help you?"

"You must be Eudora. I'm Claudia. I'm so sorry this is late." She would leave off the excuses. Apologies didn't require an explanation, and this woman didn't need to hear any of her woes.

"Thank you for bringing the food. I can take them." Eudora held out her hands.

"Are you sure? I don't mind bringing them inside." The food was heavy. She couldn't be sure, but Eudora might not have the strength to carry them, but she didn't want to insult the woman by implying she needed help.

"I can take them. I appreciate you doing this for me." Eudora's smile reached her eyes this time and shot a little light into them.

"It's my pleasure." Even if she had been a total loser who couldn't cook and then fell asleep because every time she sat down she collapsed from exhaustion.

"I would invite you in, but the house is a mess, and I'm not great company at night."

"I understand. You don't have to explain. The reheating instructions are taped to the lids. I hope you enjoy it."

"I'm sure I will. All this kindness makes the food taste better."

"The people of this town seem to care for one another." She had seen that from the moment she stood on the sidewalk, staring at the mansion, and Van had come over to offer her help. This Dining Car organization, run by volunteers to ensure residents had food when they needed it.

"You're new to town. Flora mentioned it to me. Are you here with your family? A husband or wife?" Eudora said.

"Just me. I'm here alone." Except for Talbot. Since they had arrived in Candlewood Falls, Claudia had hardly seen her. Talbot still hadn't offered any insight to whatever was bothering her, and Claudia continued to give her the space she obviously needed.

"I hate being alone. I never thought I would be. I always thought I'd have time for relationships. I always told my friends I'd take a rain check until there were no more invitations." Eudora shifted the trays in her arms. "I ended several relationships because I didn't have the time to nurture them. My family is across the country. What little there is. A brother who doesn't care about me. Probably because I had ignored him too when life was good, and I was making money and working hard. Living the dream I thought. What a fool I was." Tears spilled down Eudora's cheeks, and she wiped them away with her shoulder.

Claudia didn't know what to do. Should she grab the food? Should she hug her? Reach for a tissue? "I'm sorry. You're going through a lot." The words sounded hollow even to her. Offering a dumb apology was hardly helpful. She could kick herself.

Eudora sniffled and wiped her cheek with her shoulder again. "Life isn't fair. Is it?"

"No, it isn't." She understood that too well.

"Thank you, Claudia. I appreciate your kindness. I can't tell you how much." Eudora stepped inside and closed the door without another word.

She stood there a minute to gather her composure.

Eudora's circumstances shook her. At any second, she could be just like Eudora, sick and alone. Nothing was guaranteed. Certainly not health. No one would come to her aid either. She would also have to rely on the generosity of strangers. Back in Chicago, that was all she was to the people who lived near her—a stranger.

That wasn't the kind of life she wanted and hadn't planned on when she had started out after college. Now, she was so far down this path, she didn't know where the turnaround was.

She picked her way back to her car and slid inside. Tears filled her eyes too. She cried for what she didn't have. For what she had lost. For the foolishness in which she had believed money would solve all her problems. And for the lonely woman inside that big house with no one to share her life with.

She needed to win this competition so she could get her life in order. Money didn't buy happiness, but it bought stability, and she needed that before any changes could be made. Opportunities weren't in Candlewood Falls either. She would win, get the lump sum, and then she would find a new place to live, making it her mission to befriend her neighbors.

Answers lay in the future. A future that couldn't include Silas Wilde or Candlewood Falls. But might just include an excavator and a garden torn to shreds.

CHAPTER TEN

Walls closed in on him. Silas wiped the sweat from his forehead and looked out the kitchen window of the guest cottage. A storm had swarmed in during the last hour and knocked out the power. Thunder cracked over the little house, shaking it on its foundation and rain filled the pool below, pinging the water's surface.

Tonight, the heat pressed against his skin, confining him in this house without air-conditioning. In his cabin, he never had or needed the assistance of an air conditioner, so he was used to doing without, but here it was different.

Everything about this place was different, and he missed the familiarity of his old house. At the cabin, he could tend to his needs without the use of power. It seemed here he had forgotten how to. He didn't want to live like everyone else. He wanted to go home.

He fumbled from room to room unsure of what to do

with himself. The only flashlight he had stumbled upon didn't have batteries. Not too well thought out. He'd buy some when he went into town. He couldn't even find any candles.

His life had been like everyone else's forty-plus years ago. He and his ex-wife Patricia had bought a ranch-style house with three bedrooms and two baths nestled in Candlewood Falls and not far from the orchard so he could get back and forth without too much of a commute.

Brad and Brooklyn had come screaming into the world. His heart had filled to the brim when he saw those two little babies stare up at him with eyes as blue as his. His children. From his blood. And instantly he had wanted to protect them from all the horrors of the world. He had vowed in that hospital room nothing bad would ever happen to them.

Life went on that way for a while. A young couple raising children. Hell, he had been twenty-one when the twins were born. He was still a kid himself back then. But his fierce protectiveness of his children never wavered.

When the Gulf War broke out, something changed inside him and he couldn't explain it no matter how hard he had tried. Sometimes he chalked it up to the young man named Dave who had worked at the orchard. Dave had been barely eighteen and enlisted to fight for his country. Silas had been protective of him too. Only his protectiveness had failed to keep Dave safe. He never came back.

When Silas had tried to explain about his uncertainty of the world—especially to his ex-wife—and what it meant for his children, people stared at him as if he had sprouted another head and went about their lives.

He couldn't go about his life anymore. The world wasn't safe. And he understood that in ways he had never before. He wouldn't be sitting around waiting for bad things to happen to his family. He would be proactive. He had started simple at first. Storing extra water and canned goods in the basement of that little ranch house he had owned.

He had read everything he could get his hands on about the state of the world. Every newspaper both local and international. He spent hours in the library. So many that Huck had to come and get him more than once so he could get to work before his brothers fired him.

He had tried to make them all understand the food they ate was being poisoned with added hormones and the government was watching—everything. Huck understood, but had warned him that he was taking things too far.

All he wanted was a place where Patricia, the kids, and he could live off the land without the assistance of the power grid, the water towers, and watching eyes.

His ex-wife fought him every step of the way. She liked the ease of her life and wanted it easier. She had married a business owner, she had said. She didn't want to be married to a farmer who had lost his mind, and she wasn't about to sit around watching it happen. She sure as heck wasn't going to pick up the pieces when he had a nervous breakdown she was predicting. She threatened to leave. He told her to go, but the kids would stay with him.

She had walked out the door with barely a look back.

For any of them. He understood eventually her leaving him, but not her kids. He never had that nervous breakdown. In fact, living up the mountain had the opposite effect.

Silas grabbed his sneakers by the door and shoved them on. The storm had quieted down to a drizzle, and the thunder had rolled to the east. Fresh air would allow him to breathe again.

Thoughts of his past sat with him about as well as too many mashed potatoes and an overcooked steak did. His past had been shaken loose by the storm and the lack of power and the strange surroundings. He would take a short walk and settle down, then come back. If he still couldn't sit still, he'd take a ride to Huck's. Maybe all the commotion over there would be a good distraction from his life at the moment.

Shoving his arms into a thin windbreaker, he stepped outside. Cooler air broke up the humidity. The flowers would be grateful for the healthy drink, and he wouldn't have to water them tomorrow. If he were having that closed-in feeling during the day instead of now, he would've come out here and pruned a few bushes even if the rain pounded his head.

He headed toward the driveway and Houston Hill Road. The mansion sat dark too. He gave a quick thought to Sticks and how she was holding up without electricity, but he shoved the thought aside. She probably hating every second and calling the electric company every five minutes, demanding they show up and fix it.

Though, that image of her didn't sit exactly right with

him, and he couldn't figure out why. She had shown him more than once that her only goal was to destroy the history of this house and its connection to the town. Her fancy clothes and shoes and jewelry screamed advantages and a life where things were always done her way. An average person didn't wear diamonds that size.

When they had sat together having pizza, she had softened like a flower opening to the sun. Her face had lit up when she smiled at him from across the table, brightening his insides.

Darkness played games with the street, keeping it from him. He was unsure where the driveway met the road. His scotopic vision wasn't what it used to be. On a night like this, he could walk right into the street without noticing.

A car could come along and run him down before the driver even knew he was there.

Claudia wiped her runny nose with the back of her hand. She wished she had some tissues, but she had none so her hand would have to do, and she would clean the steering wheel later. Ever since she had left Eudora's, tears had poured like the waterfall in town. Pretty river, she had to admit. Way prettier than she had to look with her makeup smudged and her face all red and blotchy.

But for some reason, she couldn't stop crying. Stupid really. She had nothing to cry about. She was just feeling sorry for herself because she was lonely, broke, and not getting any younger. Being in her fifties wasn't all bad.

This decade brought a sense of calm she hadn't possessed in the past—except for tonight's emotional outburst. All her years had provided her with some of life's wisdoms too. She had missed the one that talked about family first, though, by being too afraid to trust that love lasted.

The storm that the meteorologists had predicted overnight apparently had changed its mind—or was determined to make a fool of the experts—and had arrived early. So early that the second she had turned out of Eudora's driveway onto the long and dark road, the skies dumped water in sheets. An unexpected clap of thunder had startled her, causing her to jump in her seat. She had knocked the phone holder from the dashboard vent, sending her phone flying to the floor. Effectively disrupting Our Lady GPS from giving directions. She had pulled over to retrieve the phone, but now the holder wouldn't stay in the vent and in her frustration and crying spell, she gave up.

Getting home had proved harder than she thought. Between the rain, the lack of visibility, and her over-whelming lack of sense of direction, she had ended up in some place called Flemington and at an abandoned or perhaps neglected and left to die outlet mall.

All she wanted to do now was go home, finish that wine, and take a long hot shower before climbing into bed. Hopefully, the attic creature had not returned because if it did, she would sleep on that stiff camelback in the den.

Her wipers worked overtime. Not because it was raining all that hard any longer but because the sensor thought it was. She played with the switch to no avail.

"Give it up, Claudia," she said just to hear something other than the classic rock station on the satellite radio.

Her warm breath fogged up the window. She couldn't catch a break. At least the house was close and so was that wine. But all the streets around town were dark too. They must have lost power. Of course they did. She should expect no less from a small town in the middle of nowhere whose claim to fame was an orchard, an alpaca farm, and a winery. Industry wasn't exactly booming in this part of the state. Probably why that awful outlet mall looked like something out of a horror movie.

She slowed her speed. Some people actually parked on the street around here and she didn't want to bump into any parked cars. A fog had rolled in, adding more complications to the ride home. She missed public transportation about now.

But she had to admit, she was glad she had brought that food to Eudora. And she would ask Flora the waitress how Eudora was doing from time to time. She would even get on the meal train again before she left.

With a sigh of relief, she turned onto Houston Hill Road. Van's house would come up first and if the power was on, she would probably notice Van's porch light. She should try to get to know her neighbor better. He seemed like a nice man.

Only a few more feet, or so she thought. Rain, fog, and a steamed window distorted her depth perception. The driveway could be further down.

Putting on her blinker, she slowed more to make the turn into the driveway. The song on the radio changed into a screaming guitar riff. Without thinking, she glanced toward the dashboard. Her car went over the lip of the driveway. Her hood was met with a thump. Someone yelled. It wasn't the singer on the radio—or her. What looked like a body bounced through the glare of the headlights.

Holy cow, she had hit somebody.

Holy fucking cow.

CHAPTER ELEVEN

Claudia threw the gear shift into park and jumped from the car. Her heart pounded in her ears, and her lungs couldn't take in air. The light spritz of rain turned back into a torrential downpour and soaked her in seconds, plastering her clothes to her skin. She wiped her hair from her eyes and tried to breathe. Her feet slipped inside her strappy heels as they filled with water from the puddle at the end of the driveway. Her knees buckled, but she caught herself on the car's hood.

"Is someone there?" She came around the front of the car. Rain sliced through the yellow-coned glow, spilling from the headlights.

A jean-clad leg was on the sidewalk, but the rest of the body was blocked from her view by the car. The leg wasn't moving.

"Are you okay?" She moved her hair out of her eyes again and knelt beside the person. A man. "Silas? Oh my God. Are you okay?"

She patted his face, his chest, his sides, his legs.

There didn't seem to be any blood, but the rain could've washed it away. She was CPR trained—well, she was once, but had let her certification lapse. She still knew what to do, except every logical thought disappeared from her mind.

"Silas? Answer me, please." How had she not seen this man? He was over six feet tall. She had glanced away for just a second and could've killed him. And his whole family would think she did it on purpose to win the competition.

"I will answer you, if you'll get off my leg and stop slapping at me." He choked out a laugh, then coughed. The rain continued to pound the ground around them.

"I'm sorry." She shifted without realizing she had kneeled down on his leg, shoving her knee straight into his thigh.

He tried to sit up, but she pushed him back down. "You shouldn't move. I can call for an ambulance. Where does it hurt?" Her phone was somewhere on the floor of the car. How had she let this happen?

"I don't need an ambulance." He tried to get up again, but she kept her hand on his chest. Heat rolled off him and over her.

"You're going to the hospital. You could have internal injuries." She straightened up, but her heel caught on a crack in the asphalt, and she fell on her butt.

Silas pushed up to stand. "Claudia, I'm fine. Did you not see me?"

"How can you be fine?" She climbed to her feet on shaking legs. Rain continued to dump on them, and she had to wipe her hair away again. Her shoe was still stuck, forcing her to abandon her shoes altogether.

"Because you didn't hit me that hard. I jumped out of the way before you could do any real damage. Were you not looking where you were going? Was there some important text that had your attention? If I hadn't been the one paying attention, you might have killed me."

"Stop being ridiculous. I wasn't going more than three miles an hour. No one dies getting hit by a car moving that slowly. The worst I would've done was give you a bruise."

"A bruise? Lady, do know how many tons that vehicle is? And you were going faster than that. You practically took that turn at top speed and jumped the end of the driveway."

"Now you're just exaggerating."

He cracked a smile, and the tension left her body in a whoosh. His hair was plastered to his head too and damn it, the man still looked good. His windbreaker was molded to his torso in a way that made her want to peel it off him.

"The inside of your car is getting soaked. Pull it in before you ruin the leather," Silas said.

"I'm sorry I hit you. I really didn't see you." Her body shook from head to toe—even her teeth chattered. A cold flush washed over her as her knees buckled for the second time.

Silas caught her in his strong arms before she hit the pavement.

"Easy there. Let's get you inside the house."

"My shoes." She lunged for them, but he held her close. He smelled like rain and cedar.

"I'll get them." He grabbed her shoes and helped her

into the passenger side of the car before hobbling around the front.

She had hurt him. Stubborn man wouldn't admit it, but her teeth continued to clatter against themselves, preventing her from arguing with him right now. She was going to loosen a filling if they didn't stop.

Silas adjusted the seat and slid in beside her. His body filled up the car and some of the fear released from her gut.

"You're in shock," he said, blasting the heat. Warm air hit her straight on, but did little to stop the chills. "When we get inside, you need to change those clothes. And I'll get a fire started to warm you up."

"I hit you, and you're trying to take care of me."

He reached over and squeezed her hand. "Lucky I know how to drop and roll." He winked.

His comment wasn't even all that funny, but laughter burst out of her mouth as if she had never heard such a hysterical thing. He gave her a quizzical glance and barked a laugh too.

Silas parked outside the garage and killed the engine. Without power, the door wouldn't open from out here.

"Are all the doors locked?" he said.

"I don't think so. I ran out in a hurry." She couldn't remember if she locked the door when she flew out to get Eudora's food. And if Van had still been in the house, he might've locked up when he left.

"I'm taking the keys and checking. We'll go in through the garage. Stay here for a second. Any chance you have a flashlight in the car?"

"Not a one. But you could use the light on my phone."

"I forget those phones can be useful. Where is it?"

"Under the seat. I think. Probably at your feet now because you pushed the seat back."

He rummaged around and found it. "How do I turn the light on?"

"How do you really not know how to use this?" She put out her hand, and he handed the phone over.

His large hand covered hers and though she was still cold from the rain and the shock, his heat penetrated her. She wanted to wrap herself in it and never let go. This man could offer her more than just a physical pleasure. She was sure of it. Around Silas, she could dream of a life where she was safe. A dangerous dream.

"You're shivering," he said.

"I'm okay." She pulled her hand away and turned on the flashlight.

"I'll hurry back."

He ran from the car, ducking his head from the rain to no avail. She pointed the vents directly on her and closed her eyes. Her head rattled as if a hundred bees buzzed around that prevented any chance of sinking into the seat and drifting off.

Silas returned and helped her out. Wet pavers chilled her feet. Water squished between her toes, but together they hurried through the garage that smelled of gasoline and wet cinder blocks. They entered the house through the dark kitchen with only the light from her phone as guidance.

"Strip," he said, wiping the rain from his face.

"Excuse me?" Hardly the kind of seduction she was used to. If this was his idea of foreplay, he could forget it.

"You need to get out of those clothes and warmed

up." He unzipped his windbreaker and tossed it in the sink. His t-shirt was also soaked and rippled against his torso. He pulled the wet material over his head and tossed that too.

Her breath caught. His pecs were still defined for a man who had to be in his late fifties and his stomach flat. He didn't have washboard abs, but it was clear he did at one time. The outline was still there even if his sides were soft above his jeans. His strong arms were corded with textured skin. He had lifted her as if she weighed nothing, which she did not, and didn't even bother trying for anymore. His long legs tapered from his trim waist.

Her stomach did a little flip at the sight of him before her. Many men had softened in the middle so much by now that their belts couldn't be seen. But this man... well, this man had benefited from his work on the orchard. In her research of Wilde Orchard, she discovered Silas could still be found in the fields grafting trees and hauling crates of apples around.

She needed to stop admiring his body while he stood only feet away from her.

"I'm not going to suffer from hypothermia." And she was not going to strip in front of him. She could find her way to her room even in the dark.

"No, but you will stop shaking, and the shock will wear off. I could call for an ambulance for you, but I'm taking a wild guess you'd prefer not to go to the hospital." He kicked off his sneakers and his socks.

"Does Candlewood Falls even have a hospital?" If he continued to undress in front of her, she might not be responsible for what she did next.

"It does not, but there's one close by. Or I can call

Dr. Trey. He's the new town doctor and young enough to be your son." He arched a brow and smirked, as if he knew what she would say about meeting a new doctor half her age.

"I don't need medical attention if you don't." She wasn't up for an introduction to the town's Doogie Howser. She'd save it for when she really needed help.

"I'll live."

"I truly am sorry. I could've really hurt you."

He waved her phone through the air. "Claudia, I'm going to light a fire in one of these fireplaces. You are going to take this gadget and make your way to dry clothes. We can talk about your bad driving skills later." He handed her the phone.

"Light the fireplace in the den." It was quickly becoming her favorite place in the entire house.

"The den?"

"The little room across the hall." She pointed in the direction of the room, but it was pointless in the dark.

"Georgette used that as an office."

"I turned it into a den. Better use of the space. Will you be able to see what you're doing?"

"Matches are in the drawer by the door. I'll be fine. When you come back down, you'll be warm."

"Thank you. What about you? You must be cold in… in what's left of your clothes." She was grateful for the room filled with shadows. Heat filled her face, and Silas would surely be able to tell.

"My jeans aren't that wet."

She doubted that was true, but hurried from the room and up to her bedroom. Once inside, she closed the door, though it wasn't likely Silas would come up here. If he had wanted to make a move on her, the car would've been a better place or the kitchen while he was removing his own clothes.

He was a decent man. He could be yelling and screaming at her for her ghastly mistake tonight. She would've been yelling at him if the tables had been reversed. Instead, he was taking care of her.

He was supposed to be her arch enemy. She wanted to dislike him so she wouldn't feel badly about doing whatever was necessary to win this dumb competition.

She pulled off her silk blouse that was probably ruined and she couldn't afford to replace, then peeled her trousers away from her legs. She draped each piece over the tub, hoping they'd dry out and be salvageable. Her shoes were still in the car. She didn't need them, wasn't even sure she wanted them any longer.

Her bra and underwear were wet too and turning her skin into slimy gills. She dumped them over the side of the tub alongside the other things and grabbed a towel to dry off. Wet girlie parts weren't exactly comfortable. She grabbed an extra towel for Silas. Wet man parts weren't going to be more comfortable either. Something that resembled desire tugged low in her belly. She tried not to picture him naked—and failed.

With dry clothes on, she shivered less, but her insides still felt cold. She couldn't help but wonder what she would have done if she had really hurt him. Certainly called an ambulance. Called his family. Then packed her things and slinked into the night.

She grabbed blankets from the closet and the pillows from the bed. That wingback sofa wasn't comfortable or big enough for both of them. This would do. Unless Silas planned on going back to the cottage.

He may have already left. She hurried from the room, using the cell phone light as her guide, wanting to return to the den. Some of the blankets dragged behind her as she navigated the grand staircase. Damp air filled the foyer and tickled her nose as if someone had opened the front door recently. She picked up her speed, expecting to find the back of the house empty and his clothes gone from the sink.

She slid into the den on her bare feet. Relief tapped her on the shoulder and said *stop your worrying*. Silas squatted down by the fireplace, feeding small sticks from a wicker basket into the flames. The room was warming up or maybe that was her. She couldn't be sure. At least the fire provided some light.

"Where did you find the wood?" She didn't remember seeing that basket anywhere.

"Georgette still had a some left on the front porch. In the right-hand corner under the overhang. You didn't see it?"

"I guess not." She had hardly gone in and out the front because that door looked unsafe. She didn't even know if the fireplace worked and had forgotten to ask Van or Dean to check it. Of course, Silas would know. His quiet self-assurance made him good at many things.

"You have a little wood left." He pushed to standing, showing off that chest again.

Lordy. He needed a shirt, or she might lose her composure and touch him. "I brought blankets."

The blankets and pillows slipped in her grasp, falling to the floor. He chuckled and ignited those laugh lines.

"I see that," he said, leaning down to pick them up, but he stumbled.

"Your leg. I did hurt you. Sit."

"Are you commanding me?" He took the blankets from her and placed them on the sofa.

"Yes. What if it's a sprain? Or worse." She could've caused a blood clot. No one gets hit by a car and doesn't feel something. He wasn't exactly the Bionic Man. Better-looking, but still.

"You don't need to worry. I won't sue you. Much."

He could sue all he wanted, but wouldn't get anything except maybe this house, and he didn't seem to want it. He just didn't want anyone else to have it either.

"Go ahead and sue, if it will get you to sit and rest that leg. I thought we'd be more comfortable on the floor than that couch. It's pretty, but not much for stretching out on. You'll come right off the edge. You're too tall for it."

"I don't think I should stay."

"But... the weather." The rain drummed on the house, as if to prove her point. She said a quick thank you for the special effect of Mother Nature because she didn't want to be alone with the power out. Not after the night she had.

"It's not so bad." He rubbed his arms.

Thunder grabbed the house with two hands and shook, helping her out again.

"You must be cold dressed like that. I brought something for you to dry off with." She rummaged through the blankets, practically tossing them in the air, until she dug out the one towel. She shoved her find at him. "I can get another if you need it."

"Thank you." He wiped his face and handed the towel back. "I can make a run for it to the house. I should be going, and let you get to whatever it is you need to do."

"You're not running anywhere with that leg tonight, even if it's nothing more than a bruise. Why get wetter? Stay here until the storm passes. There's nothing you can do over there you can't do here while the power is out." She fought the thoughts of the things they could do in the dark. It was madness to be attracted to this man.

When he didn't respond, she said, "Is something waiting for you back there?" She had never considered he might have a guest. Just because she was alone, didn't mean he was too. He had to be a catch around here. Handsome, successful, single. The available women of this town must want a crack at him.

He stared at her without a word, making her shiver all over again.

"Your... girlfriend is back at the guesthouse, maybe?" Better to find out so she really could put any and all inappropriate thoughts of Silas Wilde to rest.

"Girlfriend? Me? I don't think so. The guesthouse was closing in on me. That's why I went for a walk. Then someone came along and ran me down." His smile twitched, giving him away.

"Sounds to me like you should stay then." She was pushing too hard. She should just let him go. It wasn't as if anything was going to happen between them. He had never given her any indication he was interested in her in some kind of romantic way.

He ran a hand over his head, lingering by his neck. The space between them filled with anticipation.

"I suppose sitting in the dark with someone is better than sitting alone. And I shouldn't risk getting mowed down again." His face broke out in a wide smile, and the tightness in her chest loosened.

"Not funny." But the laugh danced over her lips anyway.

"Bad joke. Sorry." He looked down at his feet, then back up at her. "I can stay for a little while, if you don't mind having your enemy around."

"I think we can put the competition aside for one night."

She placed the pillows on the floor against the sofa and fanned out the blankets. He watched from his spot near the fire as the shadows from the flames swayed behind him. She wished for a little classic R&B just then. Maybe a little Dorothy Moore to sway to.

"Would you like to sit?" She took a spot on the floor. The room was comfortable now that she was warmer and she was with Silas. It could rain all night for all she cared. She wanted to sit beside him and find out more about this mysterious man. The competition could be damned. In the light of day, she would worry about her financial situation and how to fix it. For now, she wanted to chase a little joy.

He sat beside her, but didn't pull the blanket around him. "Are you warm enough now?" he said.

"I'm good. But what about you? Your pants… and you don't have a shirt." She couldn't meet his gaze and make mention of his state of undress.

"I'm okay. And it is kind of nice to get off my leg."

"Do you want some wine? I still have some." She pushed up to run into the kitchen, but he held her wrist.

His large hand circled it without any trouble. Heat from his skin ran up over hers.

"Sit, Sticks. Take a load off."

She sat. For the first time, she wasn't bothered by the nickname. No malice lined his words. He only smiled that slow, easy smile of his. He was used to taking it slow, she was sure, but she had never been like that, always running to the next thing, running from whatever was chasing her, and there was always something chasing her.

"Are you sure? I don't mind," she said.

"There's no rush. Let's sit for now." He arranged the blanket around her legs.

"Tell me something about yourself." She needed to fill the silence for fear she would jump up again, trying to create an activity to calm her nerves, and she wanted to know more about him.

"Like what?" He eased back against the sofa. Their arms touched. The feel of him against her started a fluttery dance in her belly.

"Like why you don't have a smartphone."

His chuckle was a low vibration. "That's a long story. But I'll give you the short version. I don't like them."

"I don't always like them either, but we live in a world where someone is always trying to reach us." Since her exit from Chicago, her phone had pinged less and less.

She was amazed at how quickly she was being forgotten. So easily replaced. Requests for lunch had practically dried up. Not one invitation to a museum opening or to an indie film premier. A telltale sign it was time to move on. Maybe the interview in New York would prove fruitful, or maybe it was time for a change. A change to what, she didn't know, but she had nothing holding her down for the first time in a long time.

"The people who need to reach me know how," Silas said, bringing her back to the present moment.

"My work was always trying to reach me. There was always a fire that needed to be put out, and I was the only one who could do it. No matter how well trained my employees were. And if it wasn't someone below me, it was someone above me, looking for favors for friends or asking about numbers and spreadsheets. It was nonstop." She had thrived on the energy of her job for decades, but in the last three years, she hadn't the energy or the desire to keep up. She had longed at times for a month off where she could recharge on a beach with no one pulling on her for one thing or another.

"You're talking about it in the past tense."

She didn't know how much to tell this man, but sitting in the dark with the only light coming from the intoxicating flames and the rain pattering against the house, lulling her, she wanted to tell him all of it.

"I quit right before I came here. Well, it was actually a mutual thing. They wanted me to go, and I knew it was time. We didn't see eye to eye on how staff should be treated." She would spare him the details of the fight on the way out the door.

When the hotel's owner, Barry Watson the Third, had told her to pack her bags and get the hell out of the hotel because she had embarrassed all of them by threatening a guest, she had said gladly. She had no desire to work for a company that endorsed harassment of their employees to make a dirty dollar. Then she proceeded to mention that Mrs. Barry Watson the Third would receive an email with footage of her husband coming out of the presidential suite at two o'clock in the morning, shoving his feet into his shoes and buttoning his fly. To which Barry Watson the Third responded by throwing a stapler at the window. She never sent the email, but watching the man's head nearly explode was worth it.

"I see. Sounds difficult."

"I would do it all over again. No one has the right to treat someone as if they're beneath them because they clean hotel rooms for a living."

Silas' brows shot up his forehead.

"What? You think differently?"

"Not at all. Everyone at Wilde Orchard from my father, who is retired but still the patriarch, right down to the new apple picker gets treated the same way. I'm a little surprised to hear you sound determined to fight for the underdog." He shifted closer to her and pulled the blanket up over his chest. Now their hips touched too.

"Why is that such a surprise?" She held his gaze. If she dared, she could easily place a hand on his thigh. She did not dare.

"It's the way you come off."

"Thanks a lot." She shifted away. If he knew about her past, he would understand, but she had so rarely shared those stories. Her secrets were better kept close. She never wanted judging eyes or a high-priced customer looking at her as if she didn't belong in their posh hotel.

"Come on, Sticks. Most times you're so made up you look like you walked off a magazine cover." He shifted back, pressing his arm against hers again.

"Because I wear nice clothes and fancy jewelry? You think you have me all figured out? Do you like that when someone does it to you?"

"I'm an open book." He arched a brow.

"I highly doubt that." He wasn't exactly one for a lot of talk. She couldn't imagine him simply spilling it for the sake of it. Most men in his age group did not operate that way. At least none she had been with.

"It's true. Ask anyone in town. They'll tell you all you need to know about me. I have nothing to hide."

"I'm not hiding anything."

"You aren't now." He turned to face her.

"What is that supposed to mean?" The room was suddenly too warm. She pushed the blanket away, but stayed close to Silas. His nose had a hint of freckles on the bridge and one right under his eye. His lips were inches away. Her fingers itched to touch his facial hair, but she fisted her hands in her lap instead.

"It means your shoulders are loose, and you're smiling more. Right now, with your hair a mess and your makeup smudged under your eyes and in those cute clothes, I can see the real Claudia. And I'd like to see more."

She swallowed the fluttery nerves that had flown from her belly into her throat.

He pushed a strand of her hair away from her face. "I've wanted to do that all night."

His touch sent shivers over her skin, driving her crazy. If he put his hands elsewhere, he would get that chance to see more of her.

"What do you want to know about me, Sticks? Just

ask, and I'll tell you." His voice was low, each word deliberate.

She wanted to know what he looked like out of those jeans, how he took his coffee, did he sing in the shower when it wasn't outside, would he call out her name during sex?

"How long were you married?" That question was on the list too.

"Too long." He held her gaze with his intense blue one. The blanket slipped from his shoulder, reminding her that he was shirtless.

"Why did it end?" She wanted to know what his skin felt like under her touch. Would it burn the way hers did?

"Because she thought she'd married someone whose touch turned everything to gold that she could spend." He played with the ends of her hair.

"And you can't spin gold?" She took a risk and traced the graying and sexy hairline by his ear. He moaned as if he had tasted something wonderful.

She almost fainted. Who was she, coming on to a man she hardly knew and who had professed himself to be her enemy? But God help her, he was the most attractive and intriguing adversary ever.

"The only thing I can spin is apples. I'll bring you some." His hands went from her ear to her neck, tracing a line down to her collarbone.

"Did you love her?" It was becoming harder to focus on what she was saying as his fingers trailed back up her neck. She tried to picture him younger and in love with some lucky woman and could imagine him stoic and solid standing off to the side, always watching. His quiet resolve would always be present and protecting.

"At first. I did. But we didn't endure."

"Why did you never remarry?" She hooked her arm around his neck and ran her fingers through the ends of his hair cut close to his neck. She could ask him about the details of his broken marriage, but they were none of her business, and they didn't matter now. She wasn't trying to capture him or worse—change him.

"Because women don't understand me." He took her leg and hooked it over his. His jeans were still damp, but she did not care that she was getting wet again.

"Do you give these women a chance to figure you out?"

"Even if I do, they don't like what they see. I'm too set in my ways for them." He ran his hand over her leg.

"What ways are that?" She couldn't stop looking at his full lips and wondered what he would taste like. Or if his chin dusted with a thicker salt-and-pepper scruff than what was on his jaw, would scratch her when she placed her lips against it.

"I like things the way I like them."

"That's not all that unusual. Don't most people like things the way they like them?" She certainly did. But she was quickly learning that she might like other things too. Like this unexpected man. He had a dry sense of humor that he was stingy with, but when he smiled, he meant it. Like he meant everything he said, and that quality was refreshing.

"Not the way I do. You like pretty things that sparkle, your comforts. I prefer simple and dull."

"You are anything but dull."

"What about you, Sticks? What's your story?" His hand stopped at her waist.

For a second, she thought of squirming out of his touch because that wasn't her best body part, but then she changed her mind. She wanted Silas' hand there and other places too.

"Just your average girl, trying to get from one place to another." Her typical answer when she didn't want to talk about her past.

"How about a real answer?" He looked right through her and she shivered again.

She closed her eyes to build some confidence; holding his gaze unnerved her at times. He rubbed his thumb over her lip, springing her eyes wide open. That simple touch fired up every nerve in her body.

"I want to know about you too," he said. "Tell me."

"Okay, here goes. I'm also divorced. Opposites don't always attract." She regretted the words as soon as she said them. Silas believed she and he could not be further apart on the spectrum of likely couples. Except he didn't know the full truth.

"Sometimes they do." His gaze landed on her lips.

Sweat broke out over her body. The room was definitely hot now. "I never remarried because I never made time for another serious relationship. I've been married to my job for a long time. I don't have any children, but I consider Talbot's son, Corbin, like my own. And I have one brother whom I don't talk to very much." The words spilled like an upended pouch of flawed diamonds. If he was attracted to her, he would surely not be any longer.

He didn't seem like the type of man who wanted a woman married to her career.

"What you're trying to tell me is that you and I are very different and we would never work out." His hand moved up her torso to her ribs.

"Probably not." She should stop this. Nothing good could come from it. Sure, there was an attraction between them. Maybe it was that thing that happened between two people when they were in a frightening encounter together. They must have confused the adrenaline from the car accident with sexual attraction.

But she didn't want to stop it completely. When he looked at her with desire swimming in his eyes, she wanted to slip her arms around his neck and get lost in those lips. Being together would only cause problems between them when one of them had to win this competition they had been thrown into. She wished she could ask Georgette exactly what she was thinking by concocting this harebrained scheme, pitting them against each other, neither of them ending up a winner in the end because someone else would get hurt.

"Silas?" She returned her fingers to his hairline, a safe place to touch and enjoy.

"Yes?" He kept his hand against her ribs, his fingers under her breast.

"I want to kiss you."

"That's good. I want to kiss you too." Those sexy laugh lines lit up and all reason wanted to leave her.

"But before we do, I need you to know I still need to win the competition. I can't afford to lose." Saying that hurt more than she had believed. She wanted him badly, but she had to be up front. Without the money, she was toast, and she was too old to start from nothing.

He eased back. His brows knit together. "That's what you're thinking about right now?"

"I don't want there to be any hurt feelings. That's all."

"Yours or mine?"

"Both."

He took her hands in his. His palms were calloused, but she liked their rough texture against her skin. She had spent too many years trying to be the soft, wealthy woman. His rugged real man feel only turned her on more.

"I want to make love to you, Claudia. I don't care about the competition right now." His deep voice vibrated low in her belly.

"Sex always complicates things."

"It sure can, but it doesn't have to. We're adults who have been around the block a few times. I know myself, and I know what I want. That's you, and I haven't wanted a woman like this in a very long time." He placed a kiss on her neck. Electricity ran over her skin in layers that could power the whole house.

"What if I get that cottage cleared out and you don't pull off the party? Will you regret this?" She leaned into his kiss.

"What if I do and you don't? Will you regret tonight?" His lips trailed her neck and lingered at her collarbone.

"I don't want you to hate me for winning." Her hands trailed up his back and his muscles flexed under her touch. He inched closer. His erection pressed against her most sensitive spot. *Lordy.*

"Let's table the competition talk until morning and enjoy tonight. When the sun comes up, we can decide what happens next." His lips found her neck again, sucking and teasing.

"Are you proposing a one-night stand?" She cupped the back of his head, holding him in place, and debated the risks involved with a single night in his arms and never again. She had not experienced in all her life a one-night stand.

"One day at a time. Slow. Take our time. We're in no rush. The future is not guaranteed. But we have tonight." He eased back and held her gaze. "Or tell me to go, and I will. Your choice."

Words formed in short angles on her tongue. One word was all it would take. He would do whatever she wanted. He was that kind of man. As little as she knew about him, she knew that much. He waited for her answer.

"Stay."

And he did.

CHAPTER TWELVE

Silas lived his life by his gut. He trusted that instinct of his when it was time to get out of his marriage and build his cabin up the mountain when everyone else told him he was nuts. He trusted his gut every planting season on the orchard when Huck or Brad raged that they were making a mistake. He trusted his gut every time it told him not to get involved with a woman.

But tonight, every fiber of his body said to make love to this woman all night long. He wanted her underneath him, calling out his name. He had meant what he said about one day at a time. No promises needed to be made. Tonight was all that mattered.

So, he kissed her. He brought his lips to hers, and she opened her mouth to him like a flower bursting through the ground in the warm sun. He wanted to devour her and tangled his fingers in that silky hair of hers, tugging to take the kiss deeper.

She gave him a little sigh which made his jeans grow tighter. Her hands explored his back, playing out small tunes over his muscles. Her petite fingers were cool against his hot skin, but did nothing to cool the heat in his veins. When she took those hands other places, he would burn up.

Her lips left his and pressed against his neck. Her tongue made circles as her hands pressed against his pecs.

"Lie back," she said with a raspy voice.

"Whatever the lady would like." He did as she asked and raised his arms over his head to give her access to whatever part of him that she wanted.

She straddled him, her hair spilling over her face like a waterfall and her center pressing against him. If she started moving those hips, he would not last.

Instead, she dragged her tongue up the center of his abdomen while she pressed his shoulders back. She created a trail of fire with that tongue and the soft touch of her breasts over his chest. His turn to sigh.

"I wanted to see what you tasted like," she said when she reached his chin and was lying on top of him. He gripped her firm ass—probably from walking around in those heels—and never wanted to let go. If he were ever lucky enough to get to do this more than once with her, he'd ask her to keep her heels on. But since she had changed into something comfortable and had left her bare feet free, he'd reserve the request. He might, however, try and find out if Sticks liked it when a man touched her feet.

"And what did I taste like?" He tilted his head down to see her and imagined she tasted like fresh fruit, sweet and ready to be pulled off the vine.

"Sweet cream."

He spun her so she was on top of the blankets and under him. She smiled, crinkling her nose. He placed a kiss there. "My turn."

Claudia could not believe she was in a house too big to be a home willed to her by an eccentric old woman, lying in the dark with a small-town orchard grower doing sexy things to her and she was letting him. And loving it.

"We need to get rid of this." Silas tugged at the hem of her shirt. She obliged him and sat up, pulling off the top.

She was glad for the dim light of the fire. It had been ages since she was half-dressed in front of a new man. She'd had a fling with a contractor at the hotel for a little while last year, but it wasn't anything special and whenever they did do it, she had insisted the lights be off.

"You're beautiful," Silas said with a thick voice.

"I don't know about—"

He pressed his fingertips to her lips. "Don't argue with me, Sticks. You don't get to be right about this one. You are beautiful."

"Thank you. So are you." Heat still climbed up her neck and settled behind her cheeks. She wanted to move things along, get back to the exploring and tasting, but Silas seemed to want to do this in his time. She shouldn't be surprised.

"Now this." Silas reached behind her and unhooked her bra with a flick of his fingers. The satiny material slid off her arms. "Even better."

His mouth ravished hers as he guided her back to the

blankets. He cupped one breast in his rough hand, but his touch was anything but. He tortured her with gentle flicks against her nipple while his tongue slid down her neck and over to the other breast.

Her back arched as he kissed and sucked. His hand moved lower and rested on her abdomen. She wanted to touch too and resumed her earlier exploration of his back. His jeans didn't have an ounce of stretch in them and didn't give at his waist.

She fumbled with the button. Without breaking away from placing wet kisses all over her, he pushed her hand aside and undid the button himself.

That was all the help she needed. The zipper released under her command, and she could free him. Finally. His mouth had sent her skin on fire and nothing but the two of them swaying as one would put it out.

He was all man in her palm, and she stroked the full length of him. Their kissing picked up speed as if a frenzy had set in. She kept up with him, teasing and taunting. Her hands all over him and his all over her. His finger dipped, finding her hottest point. Her whole body vibrated and if she wasn't careful, things would wrap up this way.

She pushed the rest of his clothes away. He released her, her breath stuck in her throat, and sat up on his knees to remove those damp jeans. His legs were as muscular as they felt under the denim. More strength. He was as solid as an oak inside and out. She could so easily disappoint this man who held the truth steadfast.

He yanked her pants to her ankles and tossed them aside. Then he lifted her foot and rested it on his shoulder. His tongue tantalized her ankle and up her calf. She vibrated all over again.

"Is this okay?" he said.

"Very." But she didn't like all the space between them. She needed him against her and hopefully inside her soon.

"Good." He didn't give her what she wanted. He continued to torture her with his tongue and lips on her leg until he sat back and took her foot in his hands.

He sat back on his heels, completely at ease in his nakedness as he worked his fingers over her foot. Slowly at first, releasing tension from the muscles. He worked his way up her leg, pausing along the way, as if exploring the curves and dips of her leg.

His hand traveled up her thigh, massaging in long strokes, each time coming closer to her heat. He switched his hand for his tongue, repeating the journey until she didn't think she would be able to stand it.

She gripped his shoulder to keep from jumping right off the mattress. That tongue had some expert experience. Age and wisdom certainly had its advantages. He returned to ravish her mouth again, then moved her until she was on her side and he was behind her.

"Is this okay?" he said between the kisses he left on her neck. His arm wrapped around her waist and held her close.

She scooted her bottom against his front. "More than okay."

His mouth descended on her shoulder. Her body hummed as he first stroked her breast, then moved his hand down her front, slipping inside her. She moaned, and his pace quickened. She gripped his thigh while he worked his magic. His hands were as expert as his tongue, and of course they would be. He coaxed plants to life with those fingers. It stood to reason he could coax her to the edge of her sanity.

"Not yet," he said, turning her so she was under him. The light from the fire reflected in his eyes. "I want this to last for you."

She wanted tonight to last because in the morning, they would go back to being competitors. She had meant what she said earlier. She needed to win and didn't want to hurt such a sweet, gentle man, but she had to look out for herself. No one else would.

"Make love to me, Silas. It's what I want." Tears threatened, and she forced them back. She couldn't have him completely. That hard truth bent her heart.

"I think I was supposed to bring this up sooner, but is birth control still an issue?"

"I have that taken care of." She wasn't exactly out of the woods in that arena, and certainly not likely any longer, but she didn't take that chance even if the men in her life were limited.

"I should've said this sooner too, but I haven't done this in a while." He drew circles around her nipple, driving her crazy all over again.

"Me either."

"Yeah?" His smile spread across his handsome face, igniting those laugh lines.

"You should smile like that more often." She ran her fingers over his jaw. His beard tickled her fingers.

"I smile when I have a good reason to, like now." He placed a kiss on her lips.

"You are an incredible man."

"I'm just a man, Sticks. Nothing special about me."

"Let's argue about that later, okay?" She reached for him.

"Fair enough."

He entered her, slowly and deliberately, the way he did everything. He took his time, setting the rhythm, as if the night would last forever. When she thought she couldn't take his unhurried quest any longer because lustful desire had her in knots, momentum built with each thrust until they were slick with sweat and could not deny the need for release.

He buried his face in her hair and laced his hand through hers. She gripped his butt and wrapped her legs around his waist, taking him in the rest of the way.

Tumbling end over end, his name fell from her lips, and her jagged breath tore from her throat.

He met her then, his hands gripping her bottom until his body stiffened, then collapsed against hers. He held her close, their hearts matching the other's frantic rhythm. Even the rain echoed the pummeling against the window, an applause for their performance, the only spectator to their show.

"Hell, Sticks, you almost killed me." He laughed in her hair.

"How long before we can have round two?"

CHAPTER THIRTEEN

Claudia blinked open her eyes. Cooler air swirled above her, but she was cozy wrapped around a sleeping Silas with the blankets covering them. Heat rolled off him, keeping her warm—and for once, not too warm. The fire was almost out. Outside the window, the night sky had cleared. Clouds moved past the moon's crescent hanging especially for her to see. Her neck complained about its current angle though. She had fallen asleep against Silas' chest with his arm under her head.

She pushed up and rolled her head on her neck, but that only made her muscles seize more. Okay, she was getting too old to sleep on the floor. Even on top of more blankets, hardwood could be a bit too firm. She hated to wake him. His face was passive with a hint of a turned-up hook to the corner of his mouth. Hopefully, he was dreaming of her and their lovemaking. She tucked the blankets around him, regretting having to cover up that sexy body, but she wanted him to be comfortable.

She threw her clothes back on and padded into the kitchen. The power was still out, but the battery-operated clock on the wall above the window with its black hands said the sun would be up in an hour. She could assemble some kind of a breakfast for them. The oven worked on gas and there had to be matches here somewhere.

When the sun did come up, she was going to have to face reality. This lovely, but dangerous relationship with Silas could not continue. He had the power to steal her heart, and she wasn't in the market for that. The competition had to be hers. She only wished she didn't like her opponent so much. Feeling guilty about doing whatever was necessary to win would do her no good. She would be riddled with guilt when he lost, though. Her method to win was underhanded, and he couldn't forgive that. Wouldn't.

He didn't understand what it was like to be alone and to rely on no one but himself. He had a family and a business. She had no one who missed her or checked in with her. She had to rely on herself for her financial independence and safety. She was out of options in the money department. She needed Aunt Georgette's estate.

She could call off the excavator and let the chips fall where they may. Now that they had slept together, maybe he would consider selling his half of the house to her so she could sell the monstrous thing along with the land to a proper business entity, allowing her to walk away debt free with a chance to create stability in her life. He had to understand the importance of ensuring her later years were taken care of.

"Couldn't sleep?" Silas stood in the doorway in his

boxer briefs and nothing else. His hair was a little messed, but the sight of him there half-naked only shoved away thoughts of ending this thing.

"Did I wake you?"

"No, but when I realized you weren't next to me, I hoped you hadn't ditched me." He padded into the room and gathered her in his arms.

She slid her arms around his waist and held him close. "The company was great, but the floor wasn't entirely comfortable."

"You can say that again. My poor back. Even in my cabin I have a good mattress." He barked out a laugh.

"Tell me about your cabin. Is it being fixed?" She traced a finger over his collarbone, knowing small touches might not be enough for her.

He brushed her hair over her shoulder. "Another time."

"Why won't you tell me about your life now? I could just ask around. Someone is bound to give away your secrets." She winked and leaned into him, pressing her breasts against his chest.

"I want to prolong the part where you decide I'm not right for you. I like you, Claudia. I think you like me too after what we just shared. You might change your mind once you find out about how I live my life." He ran his hands over her back. If he kept that up, she would have to escort him upstairs and show him her mattress.

"Why would you think I'd change my mind about you once I learned about your house?" She had no idea what his house could look like. His cabin could be a sprawling house with lots of windows and a deck with a view of a lake. Or it could be something else. She didn't care.

"Because women always do." He eased out of the embrace.

"I'm not all women." She preferred to have his arms around her, but she would honor the space he put between them. She busied herself with finding matches for the burner.

"No, you are definitely not like any other woman I've known. But you're a woman used to a house like this." He waved a hand in the air. "Better than this. I'm sure."

"Why don't you try me?" She pulled open a drawer, but found nothing that resembled matches in the gray light of dawn.

"Standing here in my underwear?" His lip curled up in a smirk.

"You could take them off." Another round of love-making would far surpass the making of tea and maybe some eggs.

"If you take off yours." His lip curled further. Perhaps Mr. Wilde had the same idea as she did.

"Stop stalling. I want to know about you. Especially if we're going to continue sleeping together." What was she saying? Not two seconds ago she was thinking about how they couldn't be together and that she was prepared to do whatever necessary to win. Now she was professing she wanted to keep this tryst alive. Well, she did, but that was beside the point.

He slid onto the kitchen chair and wiped a hand over his face. "Got some coffee around here?"

"Not instant. How about tea? I was thinking I could

make us a little breakfast if I can find the matches for the burner."

"How about we take a ride and find a diner open with coffee? There's one in Clinton on Route 22 about twenty minutes away. I think it's twenty-four hours."

She went and straddled him so their fronts met. Her arms wound around his neck. "Let's go later when the world wakes up. I'll share you then. For now, I like the darkness and just you and me in our own little world."

Because in the light of day, this might all end, and she wanted it to last for as long as it could.

He held her waist. His touch would always make her want more of him.

"Fair enough," he said, kissing her lips. "How about the tea, then?"

"Tea it is." She placed another kiss on his full lips and slid from his lap, allowing her hand to trace his torso and rest on the top of his thigh.

He gripped her hand and kissed her fingers before letting her go.

"Go on," she said. "Tell me your story." She continued her search for the matches, turning to look at him.

"A long time ago, I took my young children and moved up the mountain."

"That doesn't sound so bad. A mountain house can be very nice. Great views." Nothing in the next drawer either.

"Its only view is of the trees that surround it. The cabin is, or was, one story, but it did have a small loft. I built it myself."

"You did? Impressive. Was it hard?" Not that she

was surprised. Everything about this man screamed outdoors and rugged.

"Not really. It's only two rooms."

"Not including what?" She pulled on another drawer. Success. A box of matches.

"Including the two rooms. You could pace it in about three strides. Well, I could. You might double that with those short legs of yours." His smile bolted straight for his eyes.

"Hey." Though she knew he was joking. He wasn't a mean person. He had not said a single offhanded thing to her even when he had been pretty mad at her. A fair fighter.

"Sexy legs. Very sexy. But you barely come up to my chest."

"Now you know why I wear heels all the time. Height challenged." She continued to make the tea, filling the pot with water and lighting the burner.

"Next time we—" He hitched a thumb in the direction of the den and smiled. "I want you to wear nothing but a pair of those heels. Will you do that for me?"

"I will if you finish telling me about this cabin of yours." Imagining herself in nothing but a pair of high heels and Silas drinking her in with lust in his eyes made that ache between her legs return.

"There is no electricity. Or was now that my house is inhabitable. Or running water. Any power I had was run by a solar generator. I don't have a computer or a smartphone because I don't want to be tracked. I like my privacy, and I don't want any government agency knowing my business." He turned his face away from her.

She went back to him and turned his chin with her finger. "Are you a doomsayer?"

"You mean survivalist—and not exactly. I don't own a bunker filled with supplies and guns though I have some of both." He pushed out of the chair. "I'd better be going."

"Why? You were just getting started. I want to hear the rest."

"Because this is the part where you'll tell me something is wrong with me and how you could never be with a man who believed only bad things existed in the world."

"Is that what you believe?" She had seen her fair share of bad things. Most people weren't treated fairly either. Life, as they say, wasn't fair.

"I did once. I truly did. But with time, and having two kids to raise, I had to let go of some of it. They went to public school. I work at a place where technology is everywhere and we report our taxes and follow state rules for orchards. I have a bank account again. Now, it's more about me being used to my way of life. I like the simpleness of my cabin and the lack of complications without technology. I like my privacy." He turned to go.

"Silas, wait."

He stopped and let out a long breath. "It's okay, Claudia. You don't have to explain. I'll get my things."

"You really are the most stubborn person I have ever met. You have decided all by yourself that we won't work out, and you won't even give me a chance to respond to what you're telling me."

"What are you going to tell me? That you would live with me in my cabin? That you won't mind going outside to pee in the middle of the night? That you'll gladly give up a hot shower and space to roam in your own home? Don't bother. You wouldn't last a day with me."

No, she wouldn't. She was used to her life too and the creature comforts she had grown accustomed to. She liked the noise of the city and the tall buildings and the hustle of the people. But she liked this man too. And she wasn't ready to give up, except ultimately she had to. She could not have her cake and eat it too. Too many calories.

"I don't know what I would say, but you won't give me a chance to say anything."

"Because I've been down this road before. I'm not looking to have my heart broken." He left her alone in the kitchen.

The teapot decided it was ready to whistle now that no one wanted tea any longer. She took it off the heat to quiet it down. Silas returned wearing his jeans. His shirt and jacket were on the back of a chair. He must've moved them when she wasn't paying attention last night, too content with the aftereffects of their lovemaking to notice. He pulled on his shirt and shoes, staying quiet, keeping his gaze on his task.

Without a look back, and his hand on the door, he said, "Thank you, Claudia. I enjoyed our night."

CHAPTER FOURTEEN

Silas parked his truck in the public lot behind Main Street. All the street spots were taken, and he needed a strong cup of coffee. A high-tech gadget took up space on the counter in the guesthouse that he had no inclination of learning how to use. A good old-fashioned percolator was all he ever needed. Though, he wouldn't complain about the ease of buying a large to-go cup from Green Bean.

His leg ached some from where Claudia dinged him with the car the other night. The walk around the block might do him good, though. Warmth already coated the air. A typical summer day was ahead of them. Good for his trees and his flowers.

People already filled the tables outside Green Bean along the store's side. He waved to Lynn who worked at the post office.

"Hey, Silas," she said, tossing her long black hair behind her shoulder.

Inside the Green Bean, people filled most of those

tables too, talking in loud voices or working at their computers. Too many buzzing people to be around this early in the morning. He pressed on the muscles in his neck to ease some of the tension that built there and took a big inhale of the full-flavored smell of coffee, floating around him.

He had tried to avoid Claudia ever since he left her the other morning. He didn't want to relive what they had shared because knowing he could not have it over and over hurt like an oil burn. The two of them existing as anything more than opponents was a foolish thought. He had allowed his hankering to get the better of him.

And there she was, sitting in the corner talking with Flora from Murphy's. Flora stood while Claudia remained seated. He couldn't hear what they were saying, but Flora clapped and cheered.

"I don't usually see you here when the place is so busy," Carter said, standing next to him in line and adjusting his tie.

"Needed some coffee." He needed more than that now that he was in the same space as Claudia. He kept his back to her so he could pretend he hadn't seen her. The clapping had picked up again. Whatever Claudia had said certainly had Flora's attention.

"Must be good news," Carter said, pointing in Flora and Claudia's direction.

"Must be."

"How's it going with our new resident?" They moved up in line.

"Going fine. We don't see each other much." Because

he was hiding like a child. She looked beautiful today in a fitted gray dress. Her sunglasses sat atop her head, tucked into that soft wavy hair he wanted his hands in again if only to make her moan for him. Shit, he shouldn't start thinking about her naked while he waited to order his damn coffee.

"How are the plans for the party going?"

"I have no idea how Georgette planned this thing for over ten years. Too many moving parts. A tractor is less complicated." He had to give Georgette props. He never wanted to plan another party for the rest of his life.

"She was a feisty old lady. Reminds me a lot of Weezer and what she'll be like in another twenty years. She's planning on having the town's holiday show at the winery again this year."

"She cheats to win that spot, Carter." Weezer and Carter had been married a couple of times to each other. They had a bunch of kids, all grown, and who were friends with his two. River kids were always running around the orchard when they were growing up. Causing trouble like their mother.

"I know it. But who can stop her?"

"Someone will." He had never given it any thought before, but Georgette's place would make a good spot for the holiday show. Behind the dining room was a room large enough to hold a banquet. They could utilize the open foyer as well. Look at him, thinking like a party planner. Next someone will tell him the Earth is round. He chuckled at his own stupid joke.

"What's so funny?"

"Nothing." They came up to the counter. He ordered a black coffee and Carter ordered his drink. "My treat."

He pulled out some cash and handed the money to the young cashier who sneered at it as if she'd never seen a fifty-dollar bill before.

They waited off to the side for their drinks.

He stole another glance at Claudia. Making love to her had been the best thing to happen to him in a long time—and the worst. Time away from her was the answer to his problems.

His feelings for her spun out of control, and he needed to rein them back in. Set them right. He and Claudia couldn't last. And he had been a damn fool to forget who he was and who she was too. Sticks needed a man who owned a tuxedo and fancy shoes. Someone who would be at home at one of these garden party fundraisers, shaking hands and making deals. Not him, more comfortable in his jeans and dented boots with dirt under his nails.

Another young person with pink hair called out his name. He and Carter grabbed their drinks and a table by the door where he could make a run for it if he had to. *Coward.*

"Tell me how your plans are coming," Carter said.

"I hired the caterer. Not the one Georgette used last year. I booked my niece Petra. She has the new café in town and does a lot of catering with her chef boyfriend."

"Mav Labraccio. I watched his cooking show. As long as you're paying her, I don't see why you can't hire family."

"I figured the same thing." After five phone calls, he had given up searching for strangers and had asked Petra. She was thrilled for the opportunity and Huck was glad Silas had hired his daughter.

"What's on the menu?"

"Told her to pick. I don't care what the food is. This is the last year for this party anyway." Even if he could convince Sticks the building and the land should stay with the town, go to a family maybe, no one would be hosting that party any longer.

"What about the guest list?" Carter removed the lid from his coffee and dumped sugar in.

"Georgette had two lists. One list marked *good enough* and the other marked *when desperate*. I didn't know if that meant desperate for more money or more people. I could invite them all and sit back to see what happens."

"That's one way to do it. Probably raise more money too."

"My thoughts exactly. See? All under control." His to-do list for this event was still as long as his arm, but he felt pretty good about checking something off.

He couldn't keep his gaze away from Sticks no matter how hard he tried. He needed to see her. She fidgeted with the chain around her neck. Pretty neck. Soft skin. He could still taste her, sweet and creamy.

"Silas?"

"Huh?" Busted while he was thinking about Sticks.

"I just said I have to run. I have a client meeting. Get those invitations out in the next two days. You won't make the deadline, if you don't. And I don't care if you have to email them all."

"Email?"

"You could snail mail them, but you'll be wasting time. I know you can use a computer. So don't pretend that you can't. And the orchard has plenty because I've seen them. Or you can come to my office or the winery. Or your children's houses. Are we clear?"

"I've got it under control, Carter. Stop worrying."

"Look, I shouldn't say this, but I don't want to see that house go to a major conglomerate either. You need to win this competition so you own the house and can send her on her way. The sooner the better."

"She hasn't even touched that cottage. I don't know what she's been doing except wasting time." He had a small idea, but would never tell Carter he had slept with the enemy.

"She's a smart lady, well accomplished. Don't let her fool you."

"No way she'll win." And if she loses, she would hate him, if she already didn't because of his fast getaway. Sleeping with her had been the most out-of-character thing he'd done in ages. And when that realization had hit him while he sat in her kitchen in his underwear, he had run for the hills.

"Let's see that she doesn't." Carter patted him on the shoulder and left.

She may not win, but he wasn't in any hurry to see Claudia leave town even if things between them couldn't continue. But that was most likely what she would do. She had no interest in staying in Candlewood Falls. Another reason why they couldn't be together. He had barely left this town, and she had one foot out the door.

He had no reason to stay around the coffeehouse by himself. Time to get to his cabin and find out if the tree had been removed. Then he planned on visiting with Brooklyn and the baby before stopping at the orchard.

He also saw no need to be in that guesthouse any longer than he had to.

"Hello, Silas." Claudia stood above him. Her face was void of her warm smile, but she still stole his breath.

He slid out of the chair, preferring to have the height advantage when she glared at him as if he were a bug. "Hello, Claudia."

"I wanted to tell you there will be a dumpster on the property this afternoon. I have to park it near the stone cottage. The truck will have to drive on the grass."

"The grass is still damp from the storm. They'll leave tracks from the tires and ruin the grass."

"It can't be helped. I'm sorry. I'll tell them to be careful. And if they damage the grass, I'll see if I can replace it from the reno money." She clutched her big black bag in front of her like a shield with both hands.

"How are the renovations coming?" His nephew had been working on the house for a while now, among too many other projects. Van was likely to overextend himself and not have the house done in time. And maybe that was a good thing.

He would never deliberately sabotage Claudia, but he would be happy to take advantage of any opportunities presented to him.

"We ran into another problem in the upstairs bathroom yesterday. The pipes leaked so much there was a puddle under the shower." She wrinkled her nose.

"I'm sorry to hear that." And he was. He truly didn't want her to have extra problems.

"That's the way it goes."

He expected her to say her goodbyes, but she didn't make a move to leave.

"Is there something on your mind?" He would stand there all day, waiting for her to talk to him.

"There is. May I have a word with you privately?"

"Sure." He held the door for her. As she passed, he caught a whiff of her sweet perfume and he wanted to bury his nose in her hair. Instead, he enjoyed a view of her backside in that dress and the way her calf muscles looked as she walked in impossibly high heels.

"I walked into town. Do you mind if we head in the direction of the house?" She shifted her tote on her shoulder.

"In those shoes? Don't your feet hurt?" He was glad he wasn't expected to wear those things. His big feet would look ridiculous for one thing.

"Thank you, but you don't have worry about my feet."

"Fair enough. What's up?" He would not think about the way the muscles in her feet flexed under his touch or the way her legs felt as he ran his tongue up them.

They headed toward the lot where he had parked. He could suggest they drive the rest of the way, but he wasn't sure he wanted to be that close to her inside the truck. And she could get mad at him for making implications that she shouldn't walk in those shoes. She looked great in them, but he didn't understand how she did it.

"You had no right to leave the other night before I said what I needed to say. I don't go around sleeping with men I hardly know, so what we shared was a bit of a big deal to me."

He checked over his shoulder to make sure no one could hear them. The whole town didn't need to know they slept together. Luckily, they were past the tables outside Green Bean and no one paid any attention.

"It was a big deal to me too." Bigger than she knew. He was always slow to share his bed with a woman. Sometimes too slow and the lady would tire of waiting and move on to someone more eager.

"I couldn't tell. You ran out of the house." She kept her gaze ahead, and he wished she would look at him.

"I didn't run. I could hardly walk because of my leg." He tried for levity, but she ignored him.

"You left in a hurry. Right around the time I started asking too many questions. What are you afraid to share with me?"

"You and I don't fit, is all."

"I thought we fit pretty well." She met his gaze with a glimmer in those dark eyes.

He tried to ignore the way his body was drawn to her, but he had to agree about how they fit well while making love. When he tucked her against him, it was as if she was meant for him.

"You're planning on leaving town anyway. Let's just go our separate ways now before one of us gets hurt," he said.

They followed the road around as it bent toward the parking lot. The sun did a good job of heating up the sidewalk and boiling the humidity.

"I don't know what the future holds, but I don't like being dismissed from this thing we're sharing without consent."

"Well, I'm sorry, Sticks, but this isn't the one time you can control the situation."

"Let me show you that your life, as simple as it may

be, doesn't scare me. Isn't that what you're afraid of? That I'll see your cabin and run for the hills."

"It's not just the cabin. I'll never go with you to one of your fancy events. I won't go to a business dinner. I might not even go to the movies with you. You'll tire of me saying no all time." He could quite possibly never tire of her and her energy or the way she lit up a room just by being in it.

She stopped walking and grabbed his arm. Her heat ran straight into the center of his chest. "I've never walked away from a challenge. You don't scare me. Show me your cabin."

"Let's say for the sake of argument, I do take you there. And you even think you want to try and make a go of my lifestyle. What about this competition between us? Do you think that you and I could be in a relationship and still fight for the right to keep or sell that house?"

"Why can't you see that selling that land to a hotel chain is what's best for the space and the town? Every small town needs a revenue shot in the arm. I drove through that sad and empty outlet mall the other night. That thing died a slow death because there isn't any industry in this part of the state. Don't be so naive. It's not the nineteen fifties. How long do you think Candlewood Falls will last on only its small businesses?"

"Candlewood Falls is special. The people of this town fight for it, making it a success every day. We have new families always moving in, new businesses like that karate studio opening up, and we have bigger businesses like the orchard and the winery employing plenty of people. You don't know what's best for this town. You aren't a member of it." Anger flared in his veins as if she had insulted one of his children.

She flinched. "You will always see me as an outsider. You'll never trust me."

"I'm sorry. You are already finding ways to fit in. I saw you having a good conversation with Flora. You brought food to Eudora. If you gave this place a chance, you'd find you would fit in." He wanted her to see that for herself. If she would try to appreciate what Candlewood Falls had to offer, she would fall in love with it and wouldn't want her big city filled with dirt and noise as much as she did now.

"Silas, I think you're right. We're just too different. But what kills me is here I am, thinking about how great you look today in those jeans and the way your hair does that curl thing at the top. On paper we would never work, but I want to take you back to the house and get you out of those clothes."

"Dad." Brad's truck idled in the street next to them.

He hadn't heard Brad pull up. Had he been there long? Did he hear Claudia say she wanted to undress him? *Oh boy.*

Claudia plastered on her bright smile and walked to Brad before he could open his mouth to stop her.

"Hello. I'm Claudia. You must be Silas' son. It's nice to meet you." Claudia stuck out her well-manicured hand.

Brad shot him a questioning look. He could only manage a shrug. No point in trying to explain any of it now.

"Nice to meet you finally. My dad mentioned you

were staying at Georgette's place too." Brad shook her hand.

"Did he also mention we're sleeping together?" Claudia shot him a glance over her shoulder.

Brad choked. "Um… my father doesn't usually discuss his personal life."

"Okay, Claudia, that's enough." He took her by the elbow and led her out of Brad's earshot. "What are you doing, embarrassing me in front of my kid?"

"Kid? He looks like he's about forty. What, were you a teenager when you had him?" She tried to peer around him, but he stepped in her path.

"Twenty-one," he said to keep her from walking right around him to ask Brad.

"Wow." Her eyebrows shot into her hair.

"Stay here," he said and went over to Brad, who was still waiting. "I'm sorry about her."

"I think it's good you're… you know…" Brad smirked, tilting his head.

He held up a hand to stop him. He couldn't have this conversation with Brad. "Never mind her. Did you come looking for me?"

"Not exactly. I did want to see how you were doing. Then I saw you walking with your friend." Brad burst out laughing. "I'm sorry. It's weird knowing your dad is having sex. Not that you shouldn't. That's cool and all, but it's weird."

"No stranger than knowing your son and daughter are." Not that he thought about what his children did in that area. But Brad wasn't going to shut up about it.

"Brooklyn is having sex?" Brad feigned surprise.

He needed this conversation to end. "To answer your

question, I'm going over to the cabin now to see if the tree is gone."

"Do you want me to come?" Brad's top lip curled up. He failed at trying to straighten it back out, obviously still amused by Claudia's declaration.

"No, thank you. And don't go telling your sister or Huck or anyone, especially not Raf, what you learned this morning. I can't believe this is happening." He stared up at the sky.

"Enjoy a little unattached fun, Dad. Not every woman is Mom. I'll stop by later. Winter wants to swim in the pool. Is that okay?"

"That's great. See you."

Brad drove away with a honk and wave for Claudia who nearly jumped out of those shoes as she waved back. Brad was right; not everyone was his ex-wife, but Claudia came a little too close. Patricia had broken his heart in so many places he wasn't sure he had found all the pieces. What would Claudia do to him if she took off with the rest?

CHAPTER FIFTEEN

Claudia was drenched in sweat. How lovely the sweat would've been if her body was slick from lovemaking with Silas. But no, nothing as delicious as that. Instead, she stood in the stone cottage still filled with boxes and junk that she continued to drag out to the dumpster which had, in fact, ruined the grass.

When Silas saw the yard, he would say he told her so, and she would deserve it. But it couldn't be helped. This space had to be cleared and set up and time was running out. She should have spent every waking moment on this cottage, but she hadn't. She had turned her world upside down by falling for a man she could never have.

Even the renovations of the big house were pulling her from the task here. Van had brought her a paint wheel and made her pick out colors for all the rooms. She didn't care what color they were. They just needed to be painted. But he had insisted, and she spent over an hour deciding between summer ivory and frosted petal white.

She had no idea how long she'd been out here, but when she started, the sun sat heavy in the sky and now the mosquitos were starting to make a meal out of her skin. She had barely made a dent in this mess. Aunt Georgette had lost her mind, thinking that she could take this task on all by herself. No one could do this alone. The old woman had probably set her up to fail because she had never come around and Silas had taken care of her flowers year after year.

"Are you really throwing all that stuff out?" Silas appeared in the doorway, as if she had conjured him, filling up the space and blocking the remains of the day.

She hadn't seen him since yesterday on the sidewalk. And she wasn't sure why he was here now, but she soaked in his typical attire of jeans and a t-shirt as if she hadn't seen the sun in days. No one should have that much effect on her, but he did. And worst of all, she wanted to go straight into his arms and wrap herself against him. She needed to get it together—and now.

"It's junk. Have you seen it?"

"Sticks, for all your exposure to money, you don't know antiques when you see them." He chuckled and shook his head.

"What are you talking about? There are at least ten jars of rusted nails out there." And ten shoeboxes of receipts from the seventies for items that would long have made their way to the dump.

"Not that. That's an Edison phonograph sitting on the grass. It's worth a lot. Let me show you."

· · ·

"It shouldn't be on the grass. And speaking of the grass. You need to have those tire marks filled in by my party."

"There is nothing in the rules that says the yard has to look a certain way for the party. You just have to have the party. How is the planning coming anyway?" She had not once asked him, too afraid to hear he had everything under control.

"Don't worry about that. Just get my grass fixed and get that record player inside where it's safe."

"Don't avoid my question. Your plans aren't a secret. You can see where I am in my process. But don't go and get cocky about it. I will be done in time. I promise you that. So, spill." She hoped she would be done in time. Van continued to find projects to fix. And she hadn't expected this cottage to be so bad. She had considered canceling the excavator, because she couldn't do that to Silas after what had happened between them, but now that she had a good look at what she was dealing with, there was no way she could give up her only advantage.

It wasn't personal. She hoped he would understand that someday.

"If you want to know my plans, ask Carter. I'd invite you to the party, but I doubt you'll still be here."

"Please don't start that again. We both know where we stand with each other. You're staying. I'm leaving. You want to keep this house and all the property as is. I want to sell it."

"Whatever, Claudia. I need to go. Just take care of that phonograph. It's the least you can do for Georgette."

"The least I can do? That woman did nothing for me. The person you knew was not the person I knew. She didn't care about me and my mother at all. She only willed this mess to me to screw me one last time from the grave." And if she hadn't needed the money so badly, she would've gladly stuck her nose up at this ridiculous offer that only managed to give her heart to Silas.

"I can tell you didn't know Georgette. She might've been a tough old bird with her ways, but if she hadn't loved you, she would not have put you in her will."

"She had a funny way to show her affection."

"Some of us do. See you around."

"Silas, wait. I didn't see any record player. Could you show me?" She hadn't paid too much attention to things that were secured in a container. She only wanted to make space to move around and when she had, she found a separate area that could be used as a small bedroom.

"The wood box with the rounded top. I'll put a cloth under it." His face lit up as if he were a boy in a toy store. Those gorgeous blue eyes danced with joy. Damn it.

"I can't have help." She grabbed another box from a pile that had spent years probably climbing to the ceiling like overgrown ivy. After her hard work today, she only needed to stand on the first step of the ladder to reach the next one. The box was heavy. Probably old college text books that would need to be recycled or some other useless item that Georgette had stored for no good reason.

"Putting a towel or something under the phonograph is not helping you. I'm helping the antique collector who will be thrilled to have it. And don't sell it for a song either."

"I'll be sure to have its value assessed first. Why am I

not surprised you like antiques?" She opened the box and choked on the dust spraying in the air.

"Because you think I'm old?"

"Funny. No, because you keep talking about your life as if you live in a *Swiss Family Robinson* novel." Books were inside the wilted cardboard box, but not text books. Photo albums made of vinyl with plastic pages that had yellowed and stuck to the photos after years of being in there.

"I like the stories attached to objects that have been in existence for a long time. All the hands that have passed over a piece like that phonograph had something to say and deserved to be heard and remembered. New isn't always better."

"There's a difference between holding on to an item because it's valuable and holding on to the past. I don't live in the past. I live in the here and now." Right now, her biggest concern was money. She had lost sight of that too this past week. But no more.

"Value doesn't always equate to money either," he said as if he had read her thoughts.

"Maybe." She counted the albums, ten in all. Nothing would be valuable about these albums, but maybe someone would want the old photos. She had no idea who, but she would take this box inside and look at the pictures later over a glass of well-deserved wine.

"Maybe? The picture my granddaughter drew for me is far more valuable than any amount of money. Or watching my children live happy lives as adults. I'd trade all the money in the world to know the people I love are safe and sound."

Anger wrapped its big, ugly fist around her stomach

and squeezed. "That's easy for you to say because you have money. You have plenty of money from what I can tell. Your family owns that successful orchard and you're part owner. You don't worry about where you'll go to work or when your next paycheck is coming in. Or if you'll have a roof over your head in a month."

His eyebrows shot to the top of his forehead. He took a step forward. "Hey, hang on a second."

"No, you hang on." She put up a hand to stop him from getting any closer and short-circuiting her brain with desire. "You sit on your pedestal and judge others, especially me. You decided in one fell swoop that I had money, liked to spend money, and only cared about money because I want to sell this house and all this land to the highest bidder. You decided that I couldn't possibly care about the integrity of the place or the town because I'm an outsider who's looking for big dollar signs. But did you ever ask me my full story? Ask me why I might want the money you are so casual about?"

Her breath came out in short spurts, and she was sorry she had said all that the second her lips clamped down over the last words. She had exposed herself and felt more vulnerable now than she did lying naked underneath him.

He closed the small space between them in one stride. His large body took up the air around her. She placed a hand on his solid chest to move him back, but he didn't budge.

"Look at me, Claudia." He tipped her chin up with his finger.

"Go away." She closed her eyes.

"Not a chance. Unless you really want me to."

"I don't know what I want." She opened her eyes and held his crystal-blue gaze. She wanted to end this madness and go back to Chicago, but nothing was there for her anymore. Anywhere but standing so close to this man seemed safer. Even the city that dumped her.

"I think you do. Tell me to go away and stay away. Or tell me to stay."

"Silas… I don't know what I'm doing here."

"I think you're mad at me for not asking the right questions." His deep voice dropped further as if he told her a secret. The secret that he understood her, which he did not.

"I'm mad because you made assumptions." Assumptions she had led him and everyone to believe, but the sting was still the same.

"You said yourself money is important to you."

"Why isn't it important to you?"

"I can do with very little. Less than most people can."

"I don't understand." She didn't understand his attraction to her any more than she understood hers for him. And she didn't understand his evasiveness about his life, though she should. Wasn't she keeping the truth about her past from him?

Her life as a young woman had little to do with her life in the here and now except that she had vowed never to be that poor again, and she never wanted to be judged for coming from nothing. She had wanted the players of the corporate game to believe the game had always been hers. Silas wasn't of that world. He wouldn't judge her, but she needed that money. As long as she did, they would always be on opposite sides.

"Come with me. I'll show you where I lived until recently." Silas held out his hand.

"I have a lot of stuff to go through still." She couldn't leave now even if she wanted to, and what purpose would it serve to learn more about Silas and possibly fall harder for him? Her heart was already breaking. She didn't need to pulverize it too.

"This stuff here will hold. We'll only be out about an hour."

"All the sunlight will be gone by then." The excuses held no weight, even to her.

"I'll bring you a lamp. And I promise that won't count as helping."

She was helpless to say no to him. He lit her heart on fire just by being near her. When she left this town, she would certainly turn to ash. "Okay. For an hour."

Silas had never brought a woman to his cabin. Not the kind of woman he wanted to date, anyway. His ex-mother-in-law had been there countless times and of course, his daughter who had grown up in the cabin. His nieces had visited once or twice, but no one came to his house to hang out. When he wanted to spend time with a woman, one he wanted to sleep with, starting at her place had been easier. And before long they ended things, anyway. Usually when he refused to have them over.

Now, Claudia sat beside him in the truck. She smelled like honeysuckle and female and was driving him crazy. He kept his hands on the wheel for fear of reaching over and touching her only to have her slap him away. But he wanted her to understand all of himself, then she could decide what she wanted.

"Have you been to the orchard yet?" he said as they drove past his family's legacy.

They owned acres of apple trees where customers came to pick their own during the fall. They also had fields of other apple trees where they harvested the fruit and sold them to wholesalers. Over the years, they increased the varieties of apples they offered and added a pumpkin patch. Cars filled the parking lot and customers could be seen in the pick your own flower garden he had implemented decades ago. His heart gave a little tug. This place was in his blood.

"Not yet." She gave a quick glance in the orchard's direction, then back out the front window.

"I can give you a tour." He could bring her at night when the fireflies dashed around and the occasional hoot of an owl would be the only sound. The sky went on for miles when he would lie in the orchard, staring up at the stars that decorated the sky like the diamonds she loved so much. He wanted to convince her that his town was prettier than her city.

"I'm not much for picking fruit. I don't have the right shoes."

"What you're wearing now is perfect." He ignored the dig. He liked her in the black workout shorts that hit above her knee and the oversized orange t-shirt she had knotted at the hem. Her legs looked great in her sneakers, and she had removed all the jewelry for the work she had been doing at the cottage. Her hair was swooped up with pieces hanging around her face and neck. She was a bit of a mess with a streak of dirt on her face, but he didn't care. He wanted her natural and relaxed. Well, as relaxed as she could be while she was still mad at him.

"I was being sarcastic," she said.

"I know. I was ignoring that."

Her lips turned up, but she covered her mouth with her hand. Too late. The sparkle went straight to her eyes as well.

He turned onto the long dirt road that weaved its way to his house. He owned the twelve acres the small cabin sat on as well. The property backed up to Green Acres land and would never be built on thanks to that law. He had picked the spot because no one could build behind him ever. That and it wasn't far from the orchard. He had also wanted to be near his ex-mother-in-law who had helped him raise Brad and Brooklyn.

"Did that sign say alpaca farm?" Claudia sat up straight and pointed.

"It did. Sunnyside Up Farm. Not a great name for an alpaca farm, but I didn't name it." Better for a chicken farm, but Cordy had fallen in love with the name and no one dared to dissuade her. When Brooklyn bought it from her grandmother, she wouldn't have dreamed of changing the ill-fitting, but still cute name.

"I have blankets made from alpaca fur. They are the softest. Do they sell products made from the fur?"

"Some stuff. I can take you over there after, if you want. My daughter owns it."

"Your daughter owns it? Is there anything in this town your family doesn't own?"

"Plenty, Sticks. We aren't the Kennedys." He pulled up to the clearing where the remains of his house lay on the ground. His chest ached. The logs and the wood that had once made up his house were scattered as if something had come along and crushed it with their big foot. Only one wall with the wood burning stove still stood. Glass from the few windows glimmered in the grass from the sun's reflection. The door was broken in two.

The tree had been removed finally. Drew, the landscaper, had told him he would cut up the trunk and leave it for the wood pile, but he didn't see it.

"Oh my God. This was your house? I didn't realize it was this bad." Claudia pushed out of the truck.

"Don't get too close. There could be nails sticking up that will go straight through your sneakers." He hurried after her, wanting to keep her safe. Not that she needed or wanted that from him, but he couldn't stop himself. She was petite and often dressed as if she might break. To him, she could be as fragile as his flowers and as strong as steal.

She stopped short. "When you had said cabin I pictured something else."

Probably a two-story cabin with all the latest appliances in the kitchen and windows on all sides, and a wrap-around deck. "It's not much. Well, it wasn't much. But it served me."

"What's in that other building?"

The other building was his outdoor bathroom and a place he suspected she would not use. "The facilities," he said.

Her mouth fell open. "Are you saying you don't have plumbing?"

"No plumbing. No electricity. A small generator that ran on solar. But the generator was crushed by the tree too." And removed as well.

"Why do you live like this? Or lived because clearly you don't any longer."

"I like it."

She shook her head. "I don't get the whole tiny house movement. I watched the shows on that house network. Toilets that use compost. Or showers that double as the kitchen sink. Are you trying to reduce your carbon footprint?"

"That wasn't the original idea. But I am helping the cause. Claudia, my house wasn't as fancy as some of those homes on television."

"You don't have a television. How do you know?" She fisted her hands on her hips.

"I've seen the show." He wanted to gather her to him when her brows twisted in a way that said he was out of his mind. And maybe he was.

"You're off the grid, but not entirely. You want to live like a pioneer, but you interact with society pretty well."

"It's complicated."

"I see that. Now what? Are you going to rebuild?"

He didn't know what he wanted at the moment. Staying at Georgette's had reminded him of what he was missing on a daily basis. He wasn't getting any younger. Waking up on cold mornings and limping out to the outhouse was harder each year. Would it be so bad to have a front porch with a rocking chair to sit on? Indoor plumbing?

"I don't have a lot of options at the moment. I won't live with my kids or my brothers. I own the land so I could build something new, but it would take a long time."

"Of course you own the land. I see why your ex-wife

thought she had married Midas." She threw her hands up.

"I bought the land a long time ago when it wasn't expensive to live in Hunterdon County. There wasn't a thing out here thirty years ago. It's been built up since then. It was just a good business decision. You understand those, don't you?"

"Whatever. Why did you show me this?" She wanted to stay mad at him, but the anger started to give up its hold. Buying real estate was never a bad decision. She had never had the chance to invest that way. She had always been trying to get ahead of her debt.

"So you can see how simple I live. You asked me if money was important to me, and I said not like other people. We need money in this world. But I don't want objects. Other than this land and a stake in my family business, I don't own much. I would have sold my ownership at the Orchard to Brad as soon as he became a vice president, but he refuses to let me do it. He wants me to come to work. The only reason I agree to that is because I'm the only owner without an office. If I can't work in the fields, I wouldn't be there. I bought this land so no one could tell me what to do with it."

"So, you proved we come from different planets. You win."

"I want you to see who I really am. I'm a simple man who wants little. You want to decorate the world, and you do. You light up the room when you walk into it."

"It's a lot of smoke and mirrors." She hugged her middle.

"What do you mean?"

"Thank you for sharing this with me. I mean that.

You didn't have to show me this. We're nothing to each other. I'm sorry this happened to you."

"You're not nothing to me, but don't ignore my question. Tell me what you mean about your life being smoke and mirrors."

She leaned against the truck and brushed the hair out of her face. Behind the mountains, sunset burned the endless sky a deep red. Claudia was beautiful in the diminishing light. He wanted to cup her face and kiss her, make love to her in the grass and the aches and pains in his body be damned. When he was around her, he was thirty-five again.

"This place is beautiful. I can see why you chose the spot. Coming home to this land night after night, watching the day burn away would be enough enticement for anyone."

"True. You're still avoiding me." He didn't want to read too much into what she had said. Candlewood Falls could be working her magic on Claudia, or he could be wishful thinking.

"It doesn't matter what I meant about smoke and mirrors. Forget I said it."

"It matters to me."

"Why are you digging so hard?"

"I don't know why. Except that when I'm around you I want more and when I'm away from you I want to be with you. I shouldn't. We don't fit, but I do, Claudia. I want you."

"It was the good sex." She bent her head and took her gaze away, but a tiny smile played with her lips.

He couldn't take another second of her flirtations and went to her, wrapping his arms around her waist. He didn't have the right words to explain what he meant. He barely understood it himself. And they had the competition between them to deal with, but he didn't give a damn about that at the moment. Here, with her in his arms, the sun setting behind her, and his house in shambles, he wanted her. All of her.

He bent his head to kiss her and waited for the slap against his face, but she reached up on her toes and met his lips with hers.

His head spun as she opened her mouth without hesitation and leaned into him. Her soft breasts pressed against his chest, igniting a flame in him he never wanted put out. Her hands went up his back and rested against his neck. *More*, he wanted to say, but their tongues were as tangled as vines and talking didn't seem like the best use of his time. He wanted to touch her everywhere, especially under her clothes, but settled for cupping her bottom and pressing her closer so she could feel what she did to him.

Her hands went up his shirt, and he couldn't stop the moan from echoing in his throat when her fingers played tunes against his ribs and pecs. Her jogging shorts afforded him easy access inside with its elastic waist. He reached for her backside again and found a pleasant surprise.

He stopped kissing her and eased back. She blinked up at him with swollen lips.

"You're wearing a thong."

"I don't like panty lines with Lycra." She glanced at him through her lashes.

"Can I see it?" Just long enough to take them off her. Maybe with his teeth.

"Here? In the woods? It's been a long while since I made out in the woods."

He couldn't imagine the well put together Claudia being ravished in the woods by some guy. Unless it was in a fancy cabin with all the latest features.

"You fooled around in the woods?" he said.

"I may have once or twice." Her cheeks flushed red.

"This I have to hear."

"Later." She kissed him again and for a moment he forgot about her lying with someone else.

"We could go back to the mansion. You'll be more comfortable." It would be a long ride, knowing what was waiting for him when they got there. He could run a red light or two if necessary.

"Any chance you have something soft for the bed of your truck?" She worked that swollen lip under her teeth. He wanted to work it under his.

"You want to have sex in the back of my truck?" He wasn't expecting that answer, but if she truly wanted to, he would try. Too bad he didn't have an air mattress.

"Like we were kids." She giggled.

"It's not comfortable. Less comfortable than the floor was. Let me take you to a bed and make love to you the way you deserve."

"Silas, all I want is to feel you inside me. I don't care where we do it. The grass is fine."

He kissed her again, because all the words left him. He had nothing else to say. She could tell him later about the past life she wanted hidden from him. For now, he needed to take her as the sun made its final decent and she lay beneath him calling out his name.

CHAPTER SIXTEEN

Claudia snuggled closer to Silas on the truck bed with the night sky full of stars as their view. Cicadas played their symphony, and the air smelled of cedar with a hint of rain. Another storm might be on the horizon.

Not her smartest idea to make love in the back of his truck, but she hadn't wanted to wait and return to the house. By the time they would've arrived, she would've changed her mind. And if she and Silas weren't going to be a thing, then she had wanted one more time with him to remember him by on lonely nights. Selfish. But he had wanted her too, so that eased some of her guilt.

"Are you comfortable?" he said, stroking her hair.

"I'm good. You?" Silas had been able to scour a few blankets from the wreckage of his home. The fallen tree had narrowly missed a chest where he kept linens. The blankets softened the truck bed well enough. An extra one covered them.

"My back may never forgive me, but it was worth it."
He barked out a laugh.

"I hope so." She pushed up on her elbow to get a
better look at him. In the moonlight she could make out
his broad smile and the crinkles around his blue eyes.
She traced her finger along his strong jaw, her nails
scratching against the beard growth from the day. "You
are a very handsome man."

"You're just saying that because you let me... you
know..." He winked.

Heat crept up her neck. She had wanted his lips all
over her, and he had obliged, taking her to heights she
didn't think was still possible to get to. "Your talents are
not influencing my vision. You're handsome. Classically.
Your son is too. He looks just like you."

"Thank you. He's a good man and makes me proud.
My daughter too, of course."

A man who loved his children unconditionally. Hard
not to fall for that. Especially because her father had not
been that man. He had walked out of her life when she
was a child and never looked back. For the longest time
she had missed him, hoping he would return, but as she
became an adult, she realized she was better off without
him. Silas probably couldn't comprehend a father like
that.

"I promised to have you back in an hour. I think I
broke it." Silas pushed her hair behind her ear.

"Was it part of your plan to win the competition?"

A darkness passed over his eyes. He pushed up to sit,
holding her gaze. "Is that what you think? That I would
use you to win?"

"Of course, not. I was joking." She had been, but was she really? She was determined to do what she needed to win. If he thought sex would give him an advantage, why not use it?

Because he wasn't that kind of man. But she was that kind of person. She needed to call off the excavator. She would not sabotage this man that she cared about in order to win. She would have to win fair and square.

"I would never use you. This thing between us is separate from the competition. Hell, if you would just agree not to sell the damn house to a business, I'd let you win." He ran a hand over his face.

"You don't need to let me win. I can win all by myself." She gathered the blanket around her.

"You know what I mean."

"No, actually, I don't. You think you have this whole thing in the bag? That nothing could possibly get in your way? Of course, you do. You're the man who gets everything he wants." This man needed to see what life could be like when someone else was in control. He was used to everything working out.

"I'm not saying I'll definitely win. Stop putting words in my mouth." He pushed to stand, giving her a full view of him, and shoved his legs into his boxer briefs.

The man really was gorgeous. His muscular legs were dusted with light-brown hair. He had a good butt too which looked great in or out of those jeans. And she shouldn't be thinking any of that while they were fighting again, but God help her, she wanted him.

"Tell me, Silas. Have you checked out of life, resorting to live alone in a sparse cabin, because you don't want to risk any emotional attachment? Is that why you live up here like a hermit practically?"

"Do you avoid your problems by dressing all fancy with your shoes and throwing your money around?" He yanked his shirt over his head.

"I don't throw money around." She wanted him to see her for who she really was and was terrified to tell him. Her appearance was her armor. Except right now. While she was naked.

"Did you marry for money?"

She stared at him. "Did someone tell you that?"

"People talk."

"Who?"

"Doesn't matter. It's true, then."

She had married for money, but she didn't stay in the marriage, and she didn't take any money with her, which she was deeply regretting at the moment. If she had a few extra dimes, she would let Silas win this stupid competition. She hated this town with its allegiance to him. He could think what he wanted. He was going to anyway. What would it matter now if she told him her whole story about her poor upbringing and how hard she worked to get where she was only to fall again? Did it matter to him that in order to get a seat at the corporate table, she had to act the part? Money was the most important accessory.

"You can't win this." She rummaged around until she found her bra and thong and slid into her underwear, trying to keep the blanket in place.

"I've already seen you naked, Sticks. Don't go getting modest now." He fisted his hands on his hips. She refused to look away and give him the satisfaction of even winning this argument.

She stood and let the blanket fall. Her breasts were still exposed, only having managed to get on her thong, and gave him a full view. "You aren't going to win, Silas. I'm sorry, but you won't. Please take me back to the house. I have to clear out that cottage and show you how wrong you are about me."

He finished dressing and hopped down from the truck without a word. She donned her clothes and slid beside him in the passenger seat, keeping her gaze forward and her hands in her lap.

No one spoke on the ride back. Tension filled the space around them like fumes from bad hair spray. She looked out the window as they handled the country roads at the houses set back from the street. The only lights anywhere were from inside the windows where families gathered around tables and televisions. Family she didn't have.

She was alone. And always would be. Falling for Silas was just another big mistake in a long list of recent mistakes. She would spend the night working on that cottage and every second until she was done. She had to win. She had her heart to save.

He pulled up near the garage to let her out. She dared a glance in his direction, but he didn't turn. With her heart in her throat, stopping all the words from forming that she wanted to say, she opened the door and got out. He pulled away and parked closer to the guesthouse.

Without looking back, she went inside. Tears burned

her eyes. No time for crying now. She needed to grab a lamp and see if the electricity worked in that cottage. And if it didn't, she would need a flashlight or a lantern or something that might be in the basement of this monstrosity of a house. A house that had no business belonging to a family that didn't appreciate it. Like Silas.

He lived in some two-room hovel with no plumbing or electricity as some way to defy what so many people longed for. Growing up, she would have given anything to live in a house instead of a one-bedroom apartment where her mother slept on the couch. He stuck his nose down at an actual house. He had no idea how hard it was to go without because at any time in his life, he could have walked off that mountain and into a warm and safe home.

She took a lamp from the collection of furniture in the dining room. The house smelled of fresh paint and stung her nose. She wanted out of this place and this town that would forever make her think of Silas.

The guesthouse was dark as she crossed the lawn to the stone cottage and the dumpster waiting for her. Silas was probably sitting on the floor in the living room reading by a match. She stopped. Under the Edison phonograph was a towel. Her breath caught. She searched, hoping to find him, but no sign of Silas. She wanted to hate him. But couldn't.

"Better get to work," she said to herself and plugged in the lamp. With a twist of the switch, light flooded the small space. The terra cotta tiled floor would be lovely once it was polished and some of the grout replaced. The walls were made of colonial-era stone, but someone had installed updated windows on the two opposite walls.

The ceiling was made of wood and slanted to a point. But what was most interesting to her was the small set of four steps that led to another room and a bathroom.

Once this was emptied out and cleaned, she could renovate the bathroom and turn this into a lovely writing cottage. Or another guest cottage. Between the bedrooms in the big house and the sleeping space in the two smaller houses, plus the land, this property really could make a boutique hotel. The town's quaintness and with New York City not that far away, she was certain the rooms would rent. Her mind raced around ideas for girlfriend vacations, weekends away, even honeymoons. The property had the pool and the tennis court. Plenty to offer with the shopping and a couple of restaurants in walking distance.

What was she thinking? She needed the money. She didn't have the capital to run a boutique hotel or even the desire. She was too old to start over. But not to have to worry about answering to anyone else. To be able to make all the decisions herself. She could offer Talbot, whom she had all but ignored on this trip so far, a stable job.

She peeked out the front door. The guesthouse remained dark. Had she hoped Silas would be in the outdoor shower? Or standing in the window, looking down her way? She was pathetic. And if she even dreamed of staying, she would have to see him. That would never work out because they argued in circles. Neither one of them knowing how to get off the ride.

She moved an old sewing machine out of the way of what looked like a tall cardboard box. A garment box, maybe. The sewing machine read *Singer*. It was made of steel and built into the wood frame with old style pedals. This was probably worth a fortune too if it worked. She didn't know if Aunt Georgette sewed or if this machine had been in the family for generations, belonging to someone else. It was too heavy to move far and not fit for the dumpster. She'd have to bring that phonograph back in too just in case it did end up raining.

The garment box had her curious. She tugged at the tape which came off without too much trouble because the glue had practically dried up. The flaps fell open, revealing a long white dress wrapped in plastic. She tore at it until the dress was free and strips of plastic puddled at her feet.

A wedding dress from a bygone era. Lace over linen. A plunging back with fitted lace sleeves, and a train that would flow far behind the bride if let out of this box entirely. It smelled of dust and age. The material was a candlelight and not a pure white. She preferred the softer version and thought all brides would look lovely in the muted tone. Great for all skin colors.

She ran her fingers over the lace and tried to imagine who would've worn this. Had it been Aunt Georgette's? Oh, how she wished she had asked more questions. Paid better attention and not just to Georgette, but to the choices of men in her life. Maybe she could fall in love still, but after being with Silas, she wasn't sure another man could compare. Kind of like when she found the most expensive dress in a store that was made for her, and then everything else she tried on didn't measure up.

She turned toward the photo albums. Answers about this dress and about her family might be in there. She wanted to grab Silas and show him what she had found, but she didn't dare. He was done with her. Two people could not be more wrong for each other. They had nothing in common anyway.

But her heart ached the same.

She returned to the house and grabbed the open bottle of wine and a glass, certainly having earned it after the night she had. She would need to drown her memories as she cleared space for her uncertain future.

Sitting on the floor, she dragged over the box with the photo albums. Maybe she would score a look at the woman who wore the beautiful dress. Or maybe she would learn something about her grandmother's sister.

Aunt Georgette had married Houston Hill, the billionaire in the late nineteen forties. He had made his money in car parts. Houston had passed away in the eighties, leaving his wife a ton of money. Money she had been stingy with even now.

The first album was filled with teenage girls, sitting on cement steps in a town with no name, wearing the latest fashions of the forties. Or on the boardwalk at what must be the Jersey shore in bathing suits that remarkable resemble prom dresses of today. Claudia had seen her fair share of high school proms come through The Barry Weston. Every year the skirts climbed up the legs of the girls.

She sipped the wine and flipped pages. None of the photos explained anything to her. She wasn't even entirely sure which one was Aunt Georgette. She couldn't place the woman in her mind with her creased and dried skin with any of the beautiful young women in the photos. Age was not always kind.

When her glass emptied, she filled it again. Sitting on

the hard floor, the tile putting her butt to sleep, she grabbed another album. Time ticked around her, mocking her. She should toss everything she could carry into the dumpster and never look back. But the heaviness of the wine and the fatigue in her soul held her to the ground. Looking through the albums was research. Research for what, she didn't know.

She flipped open the cover. This album was not filled with pages of photos. Most of the pages had been removed. A pocket folder had replaced them. Inside the folder was a stack of aged unopened envelopes.

She didn't have her readers and had to hold the envelopes away from her eyes in order to see the words. Her stomach hollowed out. Each envelope was addressed in the same flowing script, always in black ink. As she flipped through each one, the handwriting became more uneven and less legible as if the hand holding the pen had grown old and tired.

She went back to the beginning of the stack. *Ms. Doris Jacobs*, her mother's name written on the white envelope, and an address that Claudia didn't remember. The postmark was nineteen eighty-four. The return address was the mansion on Houston Hill Road in Candlewood Falls. All the envelopes were the same, addressed to her mother and unopened. All marked return to sender. The last one dated six months before her mother's death.

Claudia downed more wine for courage and opened the first one. Aunt Georgette had written, asking how Doris and Claudia were, and if they would like to come for a visit. The pool was open and Georgette believed teenage girls enjoyed sunning in their bikinis. She had mentioned her friend Evelyn Wilde had a slew of boys if Claudia wanted a date. Aunt Georgette had also included a check made out to Doris. Her hands shook. How could this be?

But it went on that way, time and time again. Each letter becoming more urgent than the one before. Aunt Georgette concerned that Doris wouldn't respond. That the fight between Georgette and her sister June had nothing to do with Doris. But Claudia's mother had read none of them. Had never seen the checks that added up to a sizeable amount over the years. An amount that would've helped them. That would've kept a roof over their heads. That would've allowed her mother to stay in one place so Claudia could make friends and know what it felt like to belong somewhere. The way Silas belonged here.

She finished the wine, unsure of how many glasses she had drunk. Her head spun and a pain pulsed behind her eyes. Tears spilled down her cheeks, dropping onto a letter and washing some of the words away.

Georgette had wanted them to come. Had loved them. She hadn't let them down, abandoned them the way Claudia had been led to believe. Her mother had been the culprit and she would never know why. All this time. What had Georgette believed of her? Had she wondered when Claudia had become an adult, why she hadn't sought out her great-aunt?

She wanted to share this with Silas and hear what he thought. To show him what her life had been like, but when she stood, the cottage spun out from under her. She grabbed the wall and forced herself to sit. A slow breath kept the wine from coming back up.

In a minute, she would run across the lawn in her bare feet and bang on the door of the guesthouse until Silas let her inside. She closed her eyes to stop the spinning, but it did little to help. The wine made her limbs heavy and cumbersome. She had to get up. In a minute...

CHAPTER SEVENTEEN

"What is going on here?"

Claudia groaned. A bright orange colored the back of her eyelids. Her head pounded as if a tractor trailer rumbled through it and every muscle in her body protested against her spending the night on a tiled floor. Or was it from making love with Silas in the back of his truck?

"Claudia, are you awake? You need to get up." Talbot stood above her, holding two cups of coffee in to-go mugs. She wore a big hat and a pair of sunglasses.

"What time is it?" She pushed to sitting and held the right side of her head so it wouldn't explode.

"Time for you to get your behind in the car and go to that interview I set up for you in New York City." Talbot's singsong voice made her head hurt worse.

"Interview? Was that today?" She had completely forgotten all about the interview. She had been wrapped up in cooking for Eudora and spending time with Silas. And the cottage.

"It is indeed. Why are you sleeping out here while you have that amazing house fifty feet away with multiple bedrooms? Here. Take this. Looks like you need it." Talbot handed over a cup of coffee then removed her glasses.

The aroma turned Claudia's stomach. She handed it back. Talbot tsked her and shook her head.

"I was cleaning the cottage out and fell asleep." And reading letters from her aunt that had shed a whole new light on her existence. She could not get her aching head around this newfound information.

"More like passed out from that bottle of wine." Talbot picked up the empty bottle. "It doesn't look like you got too far," she said, turning in circles.

"There's so much stuff." She shoved the letters back in the folder, not ready to share them with Talbot. She wanted to talk to Silas about them first. If he would even talk to her at all.

With the interview today, she would lose another day working on the cottage and never finish this task in time. She couldn't afford to cancel the interview. Even if she won the competition, she had no plans to stay in town. Definitely not if she and Silas were at odds.

"Can I help you throw things out while you're in New York?" Talbot gathered some of the albums.

She grabbed Talbot's hands. "No. I don't win if anyone helps me."

"Who's going to know?" Talbot's brows creased.

"Silas Wilde will." He would notice and tell. He wanted to win too and she would be giving him too good of a chance. After their last fight, he would be looking for a way to make sure she lost.

"Ah, the eccentric and elusive Silas Wilde. I've heard about him." Talbot removed the hat and ran a hand through her hair.

"Of course you have. Everyone in this town knows that family."

"And that River family. I can't go anywhere without running into a River or a River relation. They're everywhere like locusts." Talbot checked her phone. "You need to get out of here or you'll be late."

"I have to shower and get dressed. I can't go to an interview like this. I probably have tile creases on my face that will take an hour to disappear."

"How fast can you get dressed?"

"Twenty minutes?"

"You'd better run."

So she did.

Silas walked the orchard. The fruit was blooming and soon the apples that will have red skin would turn. The trees were fuller and taller this time of year. Every season was beautiful on his orchard. There was none he liked better than the other.

If he kept moving, he wouldn't think about last night with Claudia or the fact an excavator was coming this afternoon to remove the rubble of his home. He had to be there, but didn't want to watch it, wished he could send someone else. He shouldn't be attached to that cabin as much as he was. It was a building made of wood and stone that had served its purpose and now was done with him.

The house had been his home for a long time even though the space was sparse. It had been the one place he felt most comfortable until Claudia showed up in his world. Whenever he was with her, holding her, he could be anywhere. Even in that huge house that he hadn't ever imagined living in. The guest cottage grew on him too because she was nearby. But oh, how she also rankled his nerves with her determination to prove him wrong.

The land that was his sanctuary would be filled with memories of him and Claudia in the back of his truck. He might have to sell it and build a new house somewhere else. He might have to sell the truck too. She had wormed her way into his life and into all his senses. He would never be rid of her. Not that he wanted to be. He had to be.

He turned the corner at the end of the last row of trees and headed back toward the market and offices. He would drop in on Huck and Brad before forcing himself up the mountain to his house.

Brad came around the cold shed where they stored apples for distribution. His son saw him and waved.

"Is today the day?" Brad said, pushing his hair away from his face. Sweat beaded on his forehead. The day was already heating up and slick with humidity.

"I'm going there in a few minutes."

"Do you want some company?"

"No need to interrupt your workday. I'm just watching and paying the bill." Some of Claudia's words came tumbling back. She made a reference to him not worrying about money. Was she speaking from experience? Had she struggled once in her life or was she struggling now and that was why she was so hell-bent on selling.

"I don't mind, Dad. Raf has everything under control on the operations end. Huck is on the premise and so is Sam. The orchard can do without me for a couple of hours. Let me take you to lunch after too. We'll have a beer and toast your house."

"Did you hate living in that house?" He had never asked before and might be a little late in asking now.

"Hate it? No. Was it weird? Sure. At first. I think it would've been harder as a kid if we weren't so ingrained in this town. Kids weren't likely to pick on me and Brooklyn. I would've knocked their heads in. We also had cousins who accepted us. And Cordy was the loudest about no one had better bother her grandchildren."

He chuckled at the memory of his mother-in-law shaking a fist at a school event. "I thought I was doing the right thing for us. Maybe I wasn't."

Brad arched a brow. "Are you feeling okay?"

"Why wouldn't I be?"

"Since when have you thought living anywhere but that cabin wasn't right? You were always happy here."

"I don't know. Maybe since it's been broken in pieces." And maybe since he met Claudia. She reminded him that there was some life worth living among everyone else.

"Or maybe it has to do with that fancy woman with no filter," Brad said as if he had stepped into his mind and heard his thoughts.

"Claudia is unique."

"I'd say. She seems to like you."

He shrugged, unsure of what to say.

"Do you like her?"

"We're too different." That wasn't an answer, and Brad would most likely call him on it, but he wasn't ready to give an honest answer to his son.

"I'll follow you over to the house, then we'll catch lunch. Okay?" Brad said, surprising him by not pushing for more information on Claudia.

"Lunch sounds good."

He drove over to his house which wasn't long enough of a ride for the first time ever. When he pulled into the clearing, the excavator was already parked there.

Jim lumbered down out of the machine with a wave and a smile. Jim owned a construction company and had known Silas since their late teens. Jim was a big man with small eyes that needed glasses, a small smile, but a huge heart. Would give the shirt off his back in a snowstorm if someone else needed it. They had raised their kids together, though Jim had four.

"You ready?" Jim said, sticking out his hand and pushing his glasses up with the other.

"No choice, really." He shook his hand.

"Good to see you, Brad," Jim said and shook Brad's hand too.

"Glad it's you moving all this for my dad."

Jim slapped him on the back, almost knocking him off his feet. "Did I ever tell you about the time your dad came over to my house and helped me paint the whole thing before my oldest was born? Paula wanted the house painted before the baby came, and I couldn't get it done. One call to your dad, and he was there."

"Except he spilled three gallons of paint all over your porch," Brad said, laughing.

"That was a long time ago," he said. Too long.

"Doesn't matter. It's what we do for each other. You need something, I'm there. I need something, you come. I wouldn't let anyone cart this mess away."

"I cleared out anything I wanted that could be saved." Other than that chest of blankets he might need to burn because they smelled like Claudia, and a couple of other things, there hadn't been anything worth saving.

"I'll get started." Jim turned away but turned back. "Hey, why did you want that flower garden of yours torn up?"

"What flower garden? At the orchard?" He looked at Brad for an answer.

"Not at the orchard," Brad said.

"At Georgette Hill's house. We got a request to have the flower garden torn out. Jimmy Junior was on the job, but when he saw the address, he called me, confused."

His ears rung. Claudia had called Jim to come and destroy his flowers in an attempt to win the contest? That was why she had accused him of using sex to win against her. She had been planning this sabotage all along.

"Dad, are you okay?" Brad put a hand on his shoulder.

"Did Jimmy Junior rip out the flowers?" He didn't want to know, and he needed to know. He loved that woman and she had ruined him all to sell a house.

"Unfortunately, he started. He didn't do much damage, but some of those purple ones were destroyed before he thought to call me. I said to wait until he heard from me because I was going to see you in five minutes."

"He's still there?"

"Sure. I had almost forgotten to mention it because I wasn't expecting to see Brad. I got all caught up in the old days. I'm losing my attention. Sorry about that."

"Call him and tell him I'm coming back, and he can go. I'll pay you for his time." He had to hope the damage was minimal. The party was only a few days away. He couldn't have the garden party without the damn garden. He had forced himself to plan that thing, hating every step of it just to keep Claudia from winning. He had played fair because that was the kind of man he was and she came along in her flashy high heels, determined to destroy him.

"You didn't put in that request then?" Jim said.

"Jim, why would I destroy that garden I've been working on for the past ten years?" But he knew the petite hurricane who would. He had fallen for her whole game. She didn't care about him or want to get to know him better. She had wanted to turn his head and with a sleight of hand take from him.

"Then who did?" Jim glanced between him and Brad.

"Claudia," Brad said because Silas could not say it out loud.

"Son, can you stay here with Jim until the work is done and then pay him?" He didn't wait for Brad to answer, but ran to his truck and grabbed his checkbook.

"You can pay me later." Jim waved him away.

Brad took the checkbook. "I'll take care of it. You need to talk to Claudia."

Damn right, he did.

CHAPTER EIGHTEEN

The train pulled into the Candlewood Falls station. Its brakes squealed, and Claudia rocked back and forth, standing in the aisle by the door instead of staying seated as the conductor had asked. She wanted off the smelly hot train as soon as possible. She'd take her chances with falling.

The entire day had been a disaster. Her car wouldn't start when she tried to leave for the interview in New York City, and she couldn't figure out why except the gods were against her. Talbot had to call for roadside assistance while she took Talbot's car to the train station, leaving her friend and assistant stranded. Though, Talbot said she had a friend who could come and get her.

She didn't understand how anyone lived out here and commuted to the city every day. The whole commute door to door was over two hours. Awful. New Jersey had plenty of towns closer to New York that required less traveling. No wonder the north part of the state was jam-packed.

She had also forgotten her phone in the chaos to get out of the house in time. She was pretty sure it was on the floor in the stone cottage under a photo album or box, but wouldn't entirely bet on it. Her mind had been frazzled since her encounter with Silas the night before and wasn't mending anytime soon. The aftereffects of the wine hadn't helped any either.

The train came to a complete stop. She had to wait her turn to leave the car, and it took every ounce of patience she had left not to push through the two people waiting for the doors to open. They looked like a happy couple. The man was tall and had his tattoo-covered arm around the woman. She leaned her head of dark hair against his shoulder. She said something about her café, and he replied about cooking for her when they got home. The man had used the woman's name—Petra. Nice name. Claudia had seen the man before. She was certain of it, but she couldn't place where. And she chalked it all up to that frazzled mind of hers playing tricks.

She finally descended the hot train, got in Talbot's sweltering car stuck in the sun all day, and headed home. *Home*. That was almost funny. Technically, the house was not hers yet. Well, half the house may never be hers. Either way, it wasn't a home and would never be.

Her arrival into the city had been a bit of a disaster. Hopping out of the taxi, she had scuffed the back of her brand-new patent leather heels. A pair she had never worn before and would now have to fix because, buying any more expensive shoes was not in the budget.

She had been distracted, listening to the offer from

the hotel owner. Her mind wandered from the modern office with a view of the Hudson River to renovations at the mansion. Van was almost done. The crew had worked hard to make her timeline. Not every project was perfect, but good enough to put the house on the market. The cottage was the biggest problem now, along with the letters from her aunt.

Claudia wanted to get back and reread them. Finally, she understood Georgette in a way she hadn't before and wished they had spent more time together.

The hotel owner with the bald head and beady eyes had said something about the hotel's mission and how she would be an asset to that. She had shifted in the seat, trying to ignore the tightness in her skin until she couldn't sit any longer and found herself standing by the window. She had toyed with her necklace until it broke, startling the hotel owner with her squeal.

In spite of her flustration, he had offered her the job. Three weeks ago, she would have taken it without hesitation. Instead, she had told the hotel owner she would get back to him. She had business to wrap up first. Talbot would kill her.

Claudia had hurried out of the hotel and into the blistering summer day where the air was stale and thick. The city had smelled like urine, body odor, and old garbage. She bumped into everyone she tried to pass on her way back to the train station, inciting swear words and something about tourists. For the first time, she wanted out of the chaotic city life. She tried to blame it on the hangover.

Now, she followed the county road back to Candlewood Falls with a familiarity that soothed her. Maybe a dip in the pool and a tall glass of iced tea would cool her off and settle her nerves further. No more wine for her for a while. She couldn't afford a repeat performance of last night. Once she was cooled off and a little rested, she would go back to the cottage and continue to empty it out. This time she would work all night long and at least have the cottage cleared. She still had to clean it and decorate it. Some of that furniture in the dining room would be useful.

Tree-lined streets painted a picture of a bygone time. Houses with wraparound porches sat back from the road at the end of long wooded drives. She turned right toward town.

Candlewood Falls had held on to its history in spite of an everchanging world that thought newer was better. When someone crossed the town line, they could take a deep breath and a stroll down Main Street. Instead of bumping into strangers and cursing at the blunder, the residents steadied each other, came together, and helped.

She could appreciate a little quiet country living. And though Georgette's house was in town, there was still so much property and greenery to become an oasis away from all the noise and pungent smells of the city. She slammed on the brakes.

Greenery—oh no. She had completely forgotten about the excavator. It was supposed to come this morning to rip up the flowers and ruin all of Silas' chances of winning. She had planned on canceling it but between the wine and the interview, she had forgotten to call.

Flooring it around the last turn, the car bounced into

the driveway, scraping the bumper. Silas' truck blocked her from going in all the way. She threw the car in park and jumped out, running toward the backyard. Her feet slipped in her heels, and she almost blew out her ankle.

He stood among the flowers. Some of which hung limp on thin stems. Dirt and earth mixed like a bad recipe. Most of the flowers were still intact. She breathed a sigh of relief. They might be able to salvage the party. She would replace all the flowers somehow.

"Silas." She waved as she hurried over.

He stared at her with a blank look. She expected him to be furious, throwing his hands in the air and yelling. His stoic silence startled her, but she forced herself forward.

"Let me explain—"

"Don't. There is not a single explanation for this." He crumpled a dead flower in his hand. Petals and dirt escaped from his fingers and dropped to the ground.

"I'm sorry. I meant to call it off. Talbot must've, thankfully." Not soon enough, but most of the land-scaping was intact. That had to count for something.

"Talbot? Your assistant? No, the excavator owner, who knows me well, thought this was a strange request. If he hadn't, this whole place would have been overturned."

"The landscaping still looks okay. We can fix the part that doesn't." Of course, the person driving the excavator knew him well. Everyone knew him and would know he would never dream of destroying his beautiful work. She hadn't factored in this town's loyalty to him back when she still wanted to rip those flowers out by their roots.

Her attempt to sabotage him would've failed anyway. Now, she wished she had never thought up such a horrible scheme.

"*We* aren't doing anything. There is no we. I will fix it somehow." He ran a hand over his hair. "For the first time ever, I wish I had a damn phone."

"Silas, I'm so sorry. Please know I made the call before I knew you. Before anything had happened between us." She put a hand on his arm, but he shrugged her off. Her stomach folded in on itself.

"And after you allowed me to touch you and love you, you were still planning on destroying all my hard work? Who are you?" His voice remained calm and soft and that scared her worse than if he had ranted and raved.

"I wasn't thinking clearly back when I first got to town. I just wanted to win." She wished he would yell at her, tell her what an awful person she was because she was feeling like the worst kind of person. To play under-handed that way seemed like someone else making that decision now. Now that she knew this man—and loved him.

"You still want to win. That hasn't changed." He swiped the broken flowers from the ground and held them under her nose.

"Yes, but not at the expense of hurting you. Not like this." She had to make him understand that this decision was before she fell for him.

"Funny way of showing it."

"How can I make this better?" She had fixed prob-lems far bigger than this one. There must a full-fledged landscaper in this county that could come out and put down brand-new grass and flowers for a hefty price. She could max out her credit card to do it.

"You can't, and I wouldn't let you even if you could. I realize we don't know each other that well, but I thought you might be different. That was why I took you to my house. Well, what was left of my house and my heart. Home means something to me. These flowers mean something to me, and you meant something to me."

She might be able to repair the flowers, but she had lost him for good. "How we feel about each other doesn't have to change. What if we went to Carter together and said we came to our own decisions. He doesn't have to be bound to the stipulations, if we both agree. I can help with the party. We can choose together who to sell the house to." She rambled but the words did nothing to change that empty expression on his face.

"Now you want to work together? Now you want a solution to suit us both? I can still win this whole thing, and I plan on it. Then you'll get nothing. Like you deserve." He dropped the rest of the flowers in his hand and stomped into the guesthouse.

She dropped onto the ground, not caring about the grass and dirt stains on her white suit pants and covered her face with her hands. She knew getting involved with Silas was a mistake that would cost her dearly, and she went ahead and did it anyway. Just like she went ahead and stuck up for Louisa. Instead, they both ended up unemployed. Who was she kidding? She would defend Louisa to the end over and over even though Louisa had ended their friendship. And she would fall for Silas anytime, anywhere even though she would end up in the exact same place. Alone.

"Claudia?" a small voice called to her.

She lifted her head to find Flora the waitress from Murphy's, casting a shadow over her. "Hi, Flora."

"Are you okay?" Flora took in the mess and her sitting in it.

"Been better. Is there something I can help you with or did you come looking for Silas?" She hoped Flora was on a mission for Silas. She wasn't in the mood to plaster on a smile and pretend that she cared about anything except licking her wounds.

"I was looking for you, but what happened to the garden?"

"I happened to the garden." She fisted some dirt and tossed it in the air.

"Do you want to talk about it? I'm a good listener," Flora said, adjusting her perky ponytail.

"No, thank you."

"Okay. Can I help you out of the dirt? Those pretty pants are getting stained."

"I think I'll sit here and wallow in my self-pity for a minute. But thank you for being so nice."

"Being nice is easy." Flora took a seat beside her and crossed her thin legs at the ankles. She wore denim shorts and a black t-shirt. Flora was adorable, and Claudia wished she could pull off such a casual look with that kind of ease. It would take her two hours to look as if she wasn't trying.

Claudia tugged off her patent-leather shoes and wiggled her toes, freeing them. Her feet were hot and swollen and for once she was too tired to pretend she enjoyed wearing heels.

"Are we taking off our shoes?" Flora said, laughing.

"Up to you."

"Okay." Flora kicked off her sneakers. "Sitting in the pool might be nicer."

"You know what? You're right. Let's go." She pushed herself to stand and held a hand out to Flora who clasped on to hers.

Even the grass was warm under her feet, but they crossed the yard and took a few steps to the pool. Silas had a full view of the pool from the guesthouse. She forced her gaze to remain on the clear blue water and not look up to the house. Or think about Silas' striking blue eyes.

Flora took a seat at the side, removed her socks, and dipped her feet in. "Nice," she said.

"I'll join you." She rolled up her pant legs to her knees and sat on the edge too. Her feet cooled right away in the water. She let a long sigh. "Better."

"Aren't you worried about ruining your clothes?"

"Not today." In fact, if she were alone, she might rip these pants with their lining right off and swim in her underwear.

"Okay, then. I was hoping to ask you a favor." Flora held her gaze.

"I'm not very good at doing favors for other people, but ask away." Favors had always come with a price tag which was why she didn't ask for any. But sitting beside this kind woman made her want a chance to help someone and prove to herself she was a good person, even if she made a lot of mistakes.

"We have someone else in need of help. I was hoping you could make another couple of trays of lasagna like you did for Eudora."

"You know I didn't cook that food, right?" She wasn't going to lie about it. Might as well hang out all the dirty laundry now. She would be forced out of this town in no time once word spread about what she did to their beloved Silas.

Flora waved her hand in the air and crinkled up her nose. "Of course. I don't care about that. I just need someone to give food to Rebecca. Will you do it?"

"When do you need it by?"

"Tomorrow. I know it's short notice, but we have every other night for three months covered. Her husband left her without notice two months ago and hasn't come back. She works part-time at the Walmart and has three kids she's shuffling all over the place. She could really use the help. Money is beyond tight for her, not to mention her schedule."

"Someone can't grab her fast food? I saw a McDonald's not far from here."

"Sure, someone could. But a hot meal would be nicer and something for her for a quick heat up for lunch too. Plus, it's healthier."

"Okay, okay. You guilted me into it." She wanted to say no. The cottage needed too much attention. Those letters called to her, and now she had to find a way to fix the garden so Silas wouldn't spend his life hating her.

"I wasn't trying to guilt you. If you can't do it, I understand. I just thought you might want to pitch in. You have such good energy."

"I apologize for my bad attempt at humor. I'll do it." She could sacrifice a couple of hours for a woman in more dire straits than she was.

"Eudora told me how kind you were to her. She felt

your big heart when you dropped off the food. I think helping her, helped you too. I've seen the way you have opened up since you've been in town. That's why I asked you to bring food to Rebecca. Something tells me you could use the help almost as much."

"I don't need help." That was a laughable statement. Just not one she could dispute with a total stranger.

"We all need help, Claudia. Helping others makes us forget our problems for a while." Flora swayed her feet back and forth in the water.

"What makes you think I have problems?" It was as if Flora understood her.

"Something tore through Silas' beloved garden. And there was you sitting in the dirt. I'm not a psychic, but I have an idea you may be involved somehow."

"Very observant."

Flora stood and shook the water off her feet. "I have to get going. Thank you for helping Rebecca. I'll text you her address. And if you need anything, let me know. I'm always here to help."

"Thanks. And I'll make sure Rebecca gets her food." She'd set several alarms and reminders so she didn't screw this up too.

She'd make food for a hundred Rebeccas if it would cleanse the guilt for what she did to Silas. She risked a look up to the guesthouse. The curtain in the window shifted, but she couldn't see if he was there.

Well, let him get an eyeful. She stripped out of her pants, tossed her top to the side and dove in the pool.

∼

Silas sucked in a breath. That crazy woman swam in her underwear in broad daylight with a house full of contractors a hundred feet away. She had on another one of those sexy thongs. This one was neutral in color and blended in to her skin, making it difficult to decipher if she had anything on at all. He was tempted to go straight down there and pull her from the water and wrap a towel around her, protecting her.

Except she didn't need his protecting. She had made that clear by destroying the garden. He still couldn't get his head around it. Not after what they had shared. He never took sex lightly, not even in his youth. He had plenty of opportunities to have female companionship. Single women in his age group, and some even older, made themselves known that they were available and willing even with the man in the cabin. His stake in the family orchard was almost always enough to turn a head. He wanted a woman to love him as he was. Eccentricities and all because he knew he came with a cart full of baggage.

Claudia had seemed to be the first one in a very long time willing to accept him. But she had used him, distracted him with sex so she could get a leg up. And boy, had she gotten a leg up.

He dared another glance out the window. She was doing laps with her bottom bobbing up and down. He bit back the anger toward her behaving like a teenager. She must know he was watching her and she wanted to taunt him as if she hadn't done enough damage. He wouldn't give her the satisfaction and gladly leave the property, but he would have to go past the pool to get to his truck. Or he could climb out a back window and push through the shrubbery that lined the back of the property and walk into town. He'd call Huck to come and get him. Huck would ask the least number of questions. And he would have some time to figure out how he was going to win this competition and be rid of that woman for good.

CHAPTER NINETEEN

She had made more mistakes. *Add them to the list,* Claudia thought as she mixed ricotta cheese with seasoning. When she had climbed the ladder out of the pool, with her heart pumping, and her blood surging, she had enough energy to empty five stone cottages. She came inside and decided to make the lasagna for Rebecca.

She hadn't had any of the ingredients and had to locate the local grocery store. Which wasn't too difficult except she hadn't bothered to wash the chlorine off her skin or hair and just threw on dry clothes and went out. Now, her hair stuck together in clumps because it had dried stiff from the chemicals and would probably ruin her color. She hadn't found a new salon yet and couldn't afford to go back into the city for someone with the kind of reputation she was used to. Maybe she could ask Flora where she had her hair done.

The first baking dish was in the oven. The energy seeped from her bones as if an artery had been cut. Her shoulders ached, and her back twinged every time she turned to the side. All that swimming caught up to her because she rarely did exercise like that anymore. But she had so much pent-up anger for what she had done to Silas and for what her mother had done to her.

Her mother had kept Aunt Georgette from her, allowing her to believe they weren't loved. Doris had made their lives harder than they had to be by denying a relationship with Georgette. She wanted to yell and scream for the injustice. Instead, she beat the heck out of the cheese mixture.

Why had Georgette pitted her against a stranger for what should've just rightfully been hers? Now, she was a performing monkey and had complicated everything by falling for her competitor. Oh, and the decimating of his prized garden.

She tossed the spatula into the bowl and wiped her hair away from her sweaty face. Pots and pans covered the stove's four burners. Tomato sauce streaked the cabinets. Every counter showed evidence of her inability to make a lasagna without wreaking havoc. Even the floor was dusted with shredded cheese that she slipped on. She had created more work for herself than less, all in the name of trying to be helpful.

Night had grown new again and still contended with the day's humidity. Working outside in the cottage wasn't going to happen tonight. When she was done here, if she ever finished, she had to deliver the food. Then she was going to come back and collapse. Surrender was more like it. She didn't want to finish the cottage any longer. She would bow out of the competition and allow Silas the win. Her last project here would be fixing the garden.

"Excuse me, Claudia?" Van stood in the doorway wearing his toolbelt and a lopsided grin.

"Hey. What can I help you with?" She longed for the day when the contractors were gone. Someone was always looking for her. Even though she wouldn't live here permanently, it would be nice to wander the space alone.

"I'm taking off for the night. Dean will be back this week to finish upstairs. I have some other commitments so I won't be around. The faucets for the bathroom in the upstairs hallway on the east side are on backorder. I hope you weren't planning on allowing guests of the garden party to use the upstairs for anything. We still have a lot to do on that floor."

She hadn't given the guests any thought. They would most likely want to come into the house. The dining room had been emptied of the furniture. Most of it moved to the big banquet style room behind it. The foyer and living rooms were cleared and painted but not furnished. She had spent no time thinking about decorating when her mind had been on leaving. Her den was available if someone needed to come in out of the heat. She didn't want to go in there anymore.

"We can rope off the staircase. I suppose. And what about the two half baths on this floor?" Silas would need portable bathrooms. Had he thought of that? The bathroom in the stone cottage wasn't ready either, and she doubted he would want strangers traipsing through his living quarters. Did she dare call him and ask? The dilemma would give her an excuse and show him she did care about the outcome of the party.

"They're in working order."

"Well, thank goodness for something." So much for finding an excuse to speak with Silas.

Van hesitated as if he wanted to say something.

"Is there anything else I can help you with?" She wanted him gone so she could finish the cooking and possibly have the breakdown she'd been fighting all day.

He scratched the back of his neck. "It's none of my business, but people in town talk a lot. Gossip picks up a pretty good speed here. And I did see the garden. My uncle is a good guy. He's just different. He deserves to be happy."

But not with her. She didn't know if that was what Van was implying, but he didn't have to. She could do it all by herself. She had ruined everything between her and Silas right along with his garden. "He does deserve that. And I hope he is."

"But not with you?" A quizzical look passed over Van's face.

"No, not with me. He's lucky to have so many people who care about him." She went back to mixing the cheese and hoped he'd get the hint. She could never stay in this town for very long after what she did to Silas. There would always be someone around the corner who was either related to him or knew him and it would be too hard for her to act as if she didn't care about him or feel their judging eyes on her. The woman who hurt their beloved eccentric Silas. Hard to get over that one.

"Our family cares about him a lot. You know, because he's… different…"

She didn't respond. She had nothing more to add. Silas was different and in ways she loved.

"Well, I better get going. I'm late already. See you next week."

"See you." But she doubted she would. By next week, she would be far from this town. Maybe she'd go south where it was warmer. Cold winters were getting the best of her each year. She may have loved Chicago, but she hated the brutal winds and snow. South Carolina and its beaches would be a nice change. Or Florida.

The timer on the stove went off and startled her out of her thoughts. She pulled open the oven door and was hit by the pungent, smoky smell. The brown thick cheese bubbled over the top of the dish. Another ruined meal because of the outdated Ultramatic Caloric range. It was too late to order from a restaurant and becoming too late for dinner. Poor Rebecca didn't have anything to eat because of her.

She slumped against the cabinets and had herself a good cry.

Silas was stuck. He wanted to go out, but Claudia's car blocked in his truck. Honestly, it was his fault. He had left his truck right in the middle of the drive when he had come back to see the mess the garden was in. Whether he liked it or not, he had to ask her to move the car and without a phone, he had to knock on the door.

She didn't answer. He tried again. Lights were on in the kitchen. The upstairs was dark. Had she already gone to bed? Leaving the lights on was a waste of energy and money. That woman had no concept of doing without.

She might be ignoring him. He could go in through the garage, take her keys, and move the car, but he didn't want to touch it without her knowledge. No matter what had happened, it wasn't his place to walk around her house uninvited.

Funny. It was his house too, technically. But it didn't feel like his—never would. He could insist all he wanted that a major corporation had no business owning the mansion and the property, but neither did he. He'd have to sell it to someone eventually. Until now, he had been too stubborn to see Claudia might have a point. They could insist the new owners keep the house's historic elements intact. He could have Carter look into turning the mansion into a national landmark.

He knocked a third time, but didn't wait for her to answer. He'd have to go in through the garage and get her keys. Assuming they were somewhere he could even find them. She probably had them in her oversized purse and that would be wherever she was.

Or he could admit to himself, he wanted to make sure she was okay. He had said harsh things in anger, and he regretted them. She had owed him nothing when she had arrived in town. They had been enemies then. Assuming what she had said about her feelings for him was true, they had become more than friends. He wanted to believe she had ordered the excavator before she had allowed him to make love to her.

He opened the door into the kitchen and stopped in his tracks. The kitchen was a mess and smelled like something was burning. The oven door stood open, revealing the source of the burnt food. And Claudia sat on the floor with her knees pulled up to her chest, resting her head on her knees.

"Go away," she said without looking at him.

"Are you trying out for a cooking show?" He grabbed a dish towel and removed what might be burnt lasagna and closed the oven door. His attempt at humor fell flat because she didn't budge.

"Please go away." She kept her head on her knees.

"Could I talk to you for a minute?" He shifted from one foot to the other because he'd prefer not to deal with all these emotions at the moment. He battled his own unwanted feelings.

"You made yourself clear earlier." She tilted up her head and held his gaze. Black streaks ran under her swollen, bloodshot eyes. Her cheeks and tip of her nose were red.

He didn't know how to handle a crying woman. Whenever his ex-wife had cried, he would walk out of the room. She had used her tears to manipulate him into doing what she wanted, but Claudia wasn't Patricia. Not once had Claudia expected him to put out money or impress her. She had been crazy enough to say she wanted to live in his cabin.

He sat beside her, pulling his knees up too. "I'm sorry about what I said. I shouldn't have said you deserve nothing. I was angry."

"It was honest." She leaned her head against the cabinet and looked up. Her hair hung in clumps around her face. The harsh scent of chlorine wafted off her. Her clothes were stained with tomato sauce. She had cheese on her feet.

"You're a mess."

She finally looked at him. Her brows knit together. "I realize that, but you don't need to point out how I messed up my entire life. I know."

He couldn't help but laugh. "I was talking about your hair and your clothes. Even your makeup. It's not like you to look out of sorts. I wasn't implying your entire life."

She smoothed a hand over her hair. "It's been a trying day. Why are you here?"

"I came to ask you to move your car. You blocked me in. Then I saw you on the floor, trying to burn the house down."

She snapped her gaze around. "I wasn't... oh. Ha. Ha."

"I was hoping to get you to smile." He preferred that to the crying.

"I'll move it." She pushed to stand, but he gently grabbed her wrist.

"Not yet. Tell me what's wrong."

"You don't want to hear about my problems. I've caused you enough. Let me move the car and you can stop feeling sorry for me." She shrugged out of his grasp.

"You can move the car after you tell me what's going on. What has you cooking and looking like you stepped out of one of those pictures where the women don't smile and always look... let's say off."

"A before picture?"

"Okay that. Tell me, Claudia. What's going on here?"

"Flora asked me to send food again. I wanted to cook it instead of buying it. Like the other women in town."

"You never wanted to be a part of Candlewood Falls. I'm pretty sure you don't even like it here. What's different?" He didn't dare think she had a change of heart about his little town and its charm. All she had to do was say those words and he might be able to forgive her for what she had done to the garden.

"Do you think I didn't care about you either?"

"I don't know. I want to believe you did, but then I see my garden and wonder what possessed you." He didn't even care about the party. Those flowers were important to him, and that was the part she had missed.

"I'll move my car. I have to go out anyway and buy dinner. Rebecca is counting on me." She stood and stepped around him, leaving him among her chaos yet again.

CHAPTER TWENTY

Claudia wiped the sweat from her face and tasted mud. She had tried all morning to replant the flowers that the excavator had dragged out of the ground. All she had managed was a spasm in her low back, dirt up her nose, and a graveyard of pink and purple petals.

She sat back on her heels, her knees damp from the soil. The morning sun washed the gray out of the sky with bursts of orange and yellow through the tree branches. Replanting dead flowers was a dumb idea, but she had to do something, and it was too early to go to the local nursery.

Silas' truck was not by the guesthouse. She guessed he hadn't come back last night. She had moved her car, but didn't get out of it until he pulled away. They had nothing left to say to each other. She only wanted to make this right for him. But she did wonder where he had spent the night and hoped it hadn't been in the arms of another woman, at least not until Candlewood Falls was way in her past.

It was also too early to call Carter and tell him she was out of the competition, but she would do that later today. She had sent an email this morning to the New York hotel, accepting their offer. She would be out of the house by tomorrow at the latest. Now, all she had to do was tell Talbot they had employment, if Talbot even wanted to go this time.

She washed her hands, but didn't bother with the rest. Dirt streaked her legs and covered her sneakers. Her hair was piled up on her head in a frizzy mess. She wasn't wearing makeup so she could guess at the size of the bags under her eyes because she hadn't slept much.

None of it bothered her. What she needed more than a fancy outfit was a strong coffee so she walked into town. Green Bean bustled at this early hour, residents beginning their day. She searched the crowd for Silas but didn't see him. She would probably always search for Silas even when she was in New York, knowing he would not step into that city unless his life or the life of his loved ones depended on it.

With her coffee, Claudia headed back home to call Carter before plugging Garden of Dreams Nursery into her phone for directions.

"Carter River."

"Hi, Carter. It's Claudia Jacobs. Do you have a minute?" She paced the kitchen, too overwhelmed to sit. Her uncertain future balanced on a rocky ledge. Once she said the words to Carter, there was no going back.

"Hi, Claudia. I hear the renovations are coming along well."

"Listen, about that. I'm calling to tell you I'm out of the competition. The main house should be ready to sell in time, but the cottage won't be cleaned out. I can't meet my aunt's stipulations. I've also accepted a position in New York. I leave tomorrow. Let Silas know he's won." The job didn't start for a week, but she needed to figure out a new living arrangement and she wanted to be long gone before the garden party.

"I don't understand. I thought you wanted that house so you could sell it. Hold on a second. Tell him I'll call him back," Carter said as if he had pulled the phone away from his face and addressed someone else. "Sorry. I'm back. You don't want to win to sell the house? Is that what you're saying?"

"I don't anymore. The house is more important to Silas. You'll see he gets the message?" She fought back the emotional tidal wave threatening to drown her.

"Claudia, are you sure? You can both own the house."

"I've never been more sure about anything in my life. Thank you for the opportunity." She ended the call before she burst into tears.

With that uncomfortable task out of the way, she finished her coffee. "Time to put on your big girl panties," she said to the empty room.

Claudia slid into the car and allowed Our Lady GPS to take her through the country roads of Candlewood Falls. She passed more horse farms than traffic lights. Rolling hills and acres of green filled the landscape. Her heart ached, learning to love this place a little too late.

She turned into Grow Your Dreams Nursery and parked her car in the gravel lot. Rows of flowers lined the edge of the parking lot. A greenhouse-like structure housed more flowers and plants behind the flowers. Planters of all shapes and sizes were strategically placed for a customer's viewing pleasure.

Claudia found an employee, a young lady with short bright-pink hair and brown eyes. Claudia had shoes that color pink. The young woman's red apron looked crisp and new. The nametag read Trish. Trish's gaze ran up and down her, pausing at all the places she was covered in dirt.

"Hi, Trish. I need to purchase about two hundred flowers. Preferably pink and purple if you have them."

"How many?" Trish's bushy eyebrows shot to her pink bangs. At Trish's assumed age—early twenties with that skin—Claudia would've figured a woman dressed as if she hadn't bathed in weeks wouldn't have the ability to purchase so many flowers.

"Two hundred. They need to be in bloom. We can work with the color, if needed." She should've taken a few photos of the garden, but hadn't thought of it. If the flowers didn't match very well, at least they would be there. Silas would see that she tried. "Oh, I also need to know how hard it would be to plant sod."

"When do you need all this by?" Trish pulled what looked like a thick calculator from her apron pocket.

"Now."

"Now?" Trish's gaze snapped up to meet hers.

"Trish, I'm sorry if I'm not being clear. I need a lot of flowers and I need them right now. Maybe some sod to replace the grass I ruined. Can you help me with that?"

"I think so. I just started here." Trish scratched at a scab on her arm. "Let me get my manager."

"Good idea."

Trish hurried off. Claudia wasn't entirely sure how she would plant two hundred flowers today. She wasn't a gardener and hadn't thought her plan too far ahead, but there must be someone here she could hire. She'd pay any price. That was what credit was for.

"Claudia?" The male voice froze her to the spot.

She hesitated to turn, but she couldn't disappear now. On a long breath, she faced not Silas… but Brad. Disappointment gave her a stomachache.

"Hello, Brad. How are you?" She straightened her shoulders and held her head high. She didn't want this young man to report back to his father that she was moping.

"I'm good. What are you doing here?"

"Shopping. Why do you ask?" She held his blue gaze, just like his father's. Silas was all through Brad's features especially the jawline and the nose. They shared the same body shape and height too, but Brad must also resemble his mother strongly. No doubt that Silas' ex-wife would be beautiful.

"I heard about the garden."

She tugged on her dirty t-shirt. "It was a mistake."

"Okay, we can help you." Trish hurried toward them, waving her hands.

"Help you with what?" Brad said.

"She wants two hundred flowers and sod. We have both if you don't mind a mix of flowers." Trish's face beamed. Claudia was happy for Trish who must feel accomplished. She remembered what that felt like.

"What are you going to do with the flowers?" Brad said.

"Plant them for the garden party." She forced her chin to tilt up.

"By yourself?" His surprised expression reminded her so much of Silas in that moment she couldn't breathe.

"Yes. If you'll excuse me, I need to take care of my purchase. It was lovely to see you, Brad. Please give my regards to your father." She turned away. "Trish, if you'll show me to the flowers."

She walked away, hoping Brad had moved on and would forget he had seen her here. Though not likely. He would probably hurry straight to Silas and report the news.

Well, nothing she could do about that. She had flowers to plant and sweet Trish waited.

CHAPTER TWENTY-ONE

"You can't cancel the party." Carter stood in the backyard of the Houston Hill Road house, staring at him. Carter's face was red and Silas guessed it might not be from the heat.

"I can't hold a party in this yard."

"Too bad. People are expecting to come. We've paid Petra for the food. And the band. Let's not forget the band. They cost a small fortune. And the women's shelter needs the money that people donate because they came here and had a good time. It's why we serve the top-shelf liquor." Carter threw his hands in the air.

"What do you expect me to do? The grass is torn up. The flowers are gone. Well, some of them are left. But you see my point, don't you?"

Carter loosened his tie and unbuttoned the top button on his dress shirt. "From the second I said the words you had to plan a party, you have been a gigantic pain in the butt. I knew you would be. I had begged Georgette not to do this. I said, let someone who likes people plan your last fundraiser. Just give him a share of the estate. But would that old geezer listen to me? No. No one listens to me."

"That's the problem with being a lawyer in a small town."

"You aren't going to bring up the complications of the job I've been doing for forty years, are you? Do you see me talking to you about apples?" A vein bulged on the side of Carter's neck.

"You should try and relax. I don't want you having a heart attack."

"You are not canceling that party. You will have it. And you will figure out what to do about the mess. Chop everything down. I don't care. But the party happens. And if you want to win this competition and keep Claudia from bulldozing the entire property because she sold it to a conglomerate, then you'll get it done."

"I don't want to win. I don't care who she sells to."

Carter ran a hand over his face. "What are you saying, exactly?"

"I'm saying, it doesn't matter if I win. I'm walking away from the inheritance. Let her have the whole house, the land, the other buildings, the tennis court, all of it."

"You two are driving me up the wall, you know that?"

"What do you mean? What else has she done?"

"Neither of you has a learned a damn thing." Carter shook his head.

He had learned a lot, in fact. He learned he was in love for the first time, maybe ever. The right kind of love that made the sun shine brighter and food taste better.

He hadn't seen it coming, but when it hit him, he was a goner. And it had hit him the second Claudia had hit him with her car.

"I don't know what you're talking about."

"Georgette had a whole scheme. She thought she could teach each of you a life lesson at your advanced ages. She really was off her rocker. I have to get back to the office. The party is on. And make sure you wear a jacket this year."

"What life lesson?"

Carter walked away, ignoring him. He couldn't imagine what Georgette had been up to when she sat with Carter and drew up her will. He never wanted a thing from her. Didn't need a thing either. His life had been full and complete. Until Claudia stepped into it with her fancy dresses and high heels.

He wasn't sure how the party would go off. He couldn't set up the tables where he had originally planned now that the grass had tire tracks three inches deep in it. The guests came to see the flowers, but there wouldn't be much to see. He supposed the band could still set up by the pool where the power outlets were. That didn't leave space for the guests except down near the tennis courts. And the patio by the main house. Claudia still had the ugly dumpster at the stone cottage.

Claudia. She was everywhere now. His memories were full of her making love with him, responding to him. Her lying by the pool. Upset in the kitchen. Drinking coffee in town. She had taken his dark and plain world and put her dazzle on it. He would never be the same.

Truth hit him like a sledgehammer to the skull. "I get

it, Georgette," he said to the wind. "But you could've just introduced us."

If Georgette hadn't concocted this plan, maybe he would be with Claudia right now instead of heartbroken. He slid into his truck to head over to Huck's. He didn't want to be here when Claudia returned. In a few days, she would move on, and he could breathe a little easier, but he would never be able to go back to his life. She had effectively evicted him from it.

Claudia shoved the trowel into the dirt and gave up. She had tried to plant for over an hour without much success. More flowers were in the flats than in the ground. Every muscle in her body twisted into screaming knots. She had to stop repeatedly to stretch some part of her out before continuing. The bugs made a feast of her, and she was hungry since she skipped lunch and breakfast.

This idea to fix the garden for Silas would never work and now the yard looked worse than before. The nursery couldn't offer anyone to help her today no matter how much she had offered to pay. She could be at this all night and still not be done. She would have to work straight through to the garden party and that would not work because she did not plan on being here for that.

A car and a truck pulled into the driveway, parking near the guesthouse. She had to shield her eyes from the sun to get a better look. Two women hopped out of the car. A bubble of laughter filled her chest.

Rebecca, the woman with three kids and in need of

food, walked over with gardening tools in her hand. "Hi, Claudia. Word was out you needed a hand. I love to plant flowers."

With her was Eudora, carrying a wicker basket, who still looked pale, but her smile twinkled in her eyes. "I don't know how long I'll have energy for planting, but I did pack us a picnic."

But it was the two men who slid from the truck that made the tears return. Brad came toward her with another man about his age. Almost as tall with light-brown skin, black hair, and the whitest smile she had ever seen in person.

"Hey, Claudia. I hope you don't mind, but we came to help," Brad said. "This is my right-hand man and best friend, Rafael Alvarez."

"Call me Raf," the man said, holding out his hand.

She stood on shaking legs and shook his hand. "I don't understand. What are you all doing here?"

"After I saw you today at the nursery, I knew what you were trying to do for my dad and wanted to help. You were never going to finish this big project by yourself. He deserves to have the garden party go off, but he also needs to see what you've done. He cares a lot about you."

"But I hurt him."

"Hey, we've all made mistakes," Rebecca said, donning work gloves.

"I have," Raf said, raising his hand. "Silas is like a second father to me. I wanted to help out too. And since Brad and I have some experience with planting…" Raf offered a lopsided grin.

"And you helped us." Eudora squeezed her arm.

"It's what neighbors do," Rebecca said.

"I can't thank you enough. I just wanted to make up for what I did to him. He didn't deserve that. I was desperate and foolish. But once I got to know him, I had planned on calling the whole thing off. It slipped my mind." Because of all her other hang-ups.

"We're here now and this will make my dad happy. Thank you for taking care of this for him."

"I would take care of him forever if I could."

Brad winked. "Raf and I will dig. We brought some special tools. You and Rebecca can put the flowers in the ground. Eudora, you keep the drinks flowing."

"Thank you, everyone. Your help means the world to me." For the first time, she had found a home because of Silas. The love these people had for him spilled to her. And maybe, just maybe, she had spread a little love of her own.

She picked up the trowel and carried on.

CHAPTER TWENTY-TWO

Claudia climbed into bed. She couldn't straighten her arms for the cramping in her muscles. Every part of her hurt from her hair to her toes, but inside she soared. She and her helpers had completed the garden and it was lovely. Not as nice as before, but it would do the job for the garden party. She didn't know what she would've done without Brad, Raf, and Rebecca. Even Eudora, plying them with food and drinks provided much-needed sustenance.

The room was cool thanks to a working air conditioner. She sunk into the mattress and closed her eyes. In the morning, she'd pack, but for now she would bask in the knowledge she had set things right for Silas. Maybe now he would forgive her. Having Brad's stamp of approval wouldn't hurt. She would miss them all.

A loud bang vibrated outside as if a heavy object slammed into metal. She sat up. Another crash against metal. It was almost midnight. Who was out there, making so much noise? She doubted it was Van.

Slipping from bed, she went to the window and pushed the curtain back. A gasp stuck in her throat. Another vibrating crash was accompanied by a loud curse word. She shoved her feet into sneakers and hurried to the backyard.

The night air was still warm and sticky. That didn't seem to stop what was happening at the cottage. She navigated the stone steps, trying not to slip on the dew collecting.

"Are you crazy? What are you doing out here at this time of night?" She pulled her dressing gown closed.

Silas stopped with a box midair. His chest heaved from exertion. Sweat slicked his brow and soaked through his t-shirt, but he was still incredibly handsome.

"What's it look like I'm doing?" He tossed it in the dumpster, creating more banging against metal noises.

"It looks like you've lost your mind. You're making a ruckus which I'm sure will upset the neighbors, and I think you might give yourself a hernia, throwing heavy stuff around like that."

"Nice outfit, Sticks." He wagged his brows.

She glanced at her silk gown that came to her knees and covered the matching shorts and tank top underneath. She wasn't wearing a bra and he could probably tell.

"Never mind my sleepwear. Please stop, Silas. You don't have to do that."

"I know I don't. But I want you to win." He tossed another box.

"I told Carter I was out. The house is yours. You win." She wished he would not throw any more boxes. She didn't want to have to take him to the hospital in the middle of the night. She had told Brad she would take care of his father if she could, not send him into traction.

He put a box down and sat on it, running a hand over his face. "I don't want to win."

"Well, you did." She dragged another box over and sat beside him. He smelled like cedar and all male.

"You keep the house, Claudia. I don't want it."

"I don't either. It means more to you." The house meant something to her now too, but he deserved to do with it whatever he wanted. If she couldn't have Silas, she didn't want the house or the town.

"Are you going to argue with me about this too?" he said.

"You bet your ass I am. You were right about this place." She soaked in the view. At night, the house was more beautiful. Once the front was fixed up, she would be a sight. The kind of place people would come for miles to see.

"You think it should stay like it is?" He gave her a sideways glance.

"That or a private boutique hotel would be nice too. You'll decide. Why are you clearing out the cottage?"

"I saw the garden when I came home." He chuckled. "Do you know why this is home to me?"

"Because your cabin was destroyed by a big tree?"

He barked out a laugh. She loved the way he laughed. "No, woman. Because this is where you are."

"Silas, you don't have to say that."

He took her hand in his rough and calloused one. Never again would she look at a man in a suit with soft skin and think that was attractive. Silas had ruined her for other men. They would not stand a chance. She was going to be alone for a long time.

"I mean it, Sticks. Thank you for fixing the garden. You did a great job."

"I had help." Images of the afternoon popped into her head, all of them laughing and sharing stories. She had made a friend in Rebecca and Eudora. They had promised to keep in touch.

"I heard."

"Of course you did." She wasn't surprised their little adventure had made its way to Silas. If she had been Brad, she would've told Silas too.

"Raf told me. He can't keep a secret. We don't hold it against him." Silas rubbed his thumb over the top of her hand.

She hadn't expected that. "So, you decided to empty the cottage because I tried to right my mistake?"

"When I saw it, I had to help you too. I had already told Carter I didn't want to win the competition. I thought I could see to it that you would."

"We're something, us two."

"Are we something?" he said, holding her gaze.

"I found letters from my aunt. She wasn't the woman I thought she was." If she had the chance, she would show Silas the letters, but she didn't want to get her hopes up. They were just talking under the stars on a pretty night. He wasn't promising her anything.

"She was unusual. That's for sure. I figured out why she designed this elaborate plan for us."

"Really? Please enlighten me."

"She was playing matchmaker." His face broke out in a big smile that reached his eyes.

"What? Crazy old lady. Wouldn't it have been easier to say, *hey, Silas, let me introduce you to my long-lost niece*?"

"It would've, but that would not have been Georgette's style. She made everyone around her jump through hoops."

"It almost worked." She eased her hand back.

"Almost?" He leaned closer and ran a finger down her arm, sending chills over her hot skin.

"It's been a very long day, and I'm exhausted. Please don't tease me."

He cupped her face. "No teasing here, Sticks. I've fallen for you, shoes and all. If you can handle a grouchy old guy too set in his ways for his own good, then I'm yours for as long as you'll have me."

"You're not still mad about the garden?"

"Just promise me when you get mad at me for leaving the toilet seat up, you won't bulldoze my orchard." He choked out another laugh.

She threw her arms around his neck and kissed his rugged face. "I love you, Silas. All of you."

"That's good because I love you too. No more sleeping without you. I want to wake up beside you every morning and go to sleep with you every night. And in a house with electricity and indoor plumbing." He wrapped his arms around her waist and kissed her until her head spun.

"You'd come back to town for me?"

"I would go anywhere for you." He kissed her again. She would never grow tired of kissing this man.

She eased back. "I don't have anywhere to live."

"We have that giant house." He tilted his chin the direction of the mansion.

"Too big. What about the guesthouse?"

"What are we going to do with the mansion?"

"Have you ever wanted to run a hotel?" She could picture it now, the two of them working side by side. She would deal with the guests and the day-to-day operations. He would take care of the garden and love her every day. With the lump sum inheritance, it might be enough to make a few more renovations.

"I'm not a hotel guy. That's more your thing."

"I would need a good landscaper."

"If I can stay outside and keep my job at the orchard, then you have yourself a deal."

"Kiss me to seal it." She pressed her breasts against his chest, wanting more than just to kiss him tonight.

"I'll kiss you for any reason at all, Sticks. And for as long as I am allowed. You stole my heart and I don't want it back."

"Let's go inside."

He stood and held out his hand. They walked away from the mansion with its rooms and space and climbed the stairs to the guesthouse. They climbed the stairs home.

CHAPTER TWENTY-THREE

Two weeks later.

Candlewood Falls held their annual summer festival at the park behind the municipal building. Claudia hadn't been to a town event like this ever in her life. Opening presents on Christmas morning held a similar sensation.

The park was full of people in all shapes, sizes, and ages. Parents pushing strollers, teenagers riding skateboards. There were store vendors and food vendors. Some businesses offered demonstrations and music piped in over a PA system. A clown twisted balloons into animal shapes.

"After the three-legged race, we'll get some ice cream and do whatever activities you want. It's your day." Silas slid his hand around hers as they made their way to the start of the race.

Most everyone in town had heard by now about the two of them. They had arrived at the garden party as a couple. Silas wore a navy-blue jacket, a soft button-down shirt, and a pair of jeans. She could barely wait to get the jacket off him later that night. She had opted for a short, square heel so as not to sink in the grass. Any heel-wearing girl would know to stay away from the spikes when the event is on the lawn.

She loved having people glance at them as they passed. Some waved. Some whispered behind their hands. But she wanted to shout to the world that she had won the prize. Silas Wilde's heart.

"I love the idea of the new boutique hotel hosting the holiday showcase," she said.

Silas had explained to her about the annual winter event the town held along with the Victorian House Christmas tour where homes in town allowed people to come and view their decorations. He had mentioned his niece Lacey always did a stunning job with her bed and breakfast. Claudia couldn't wait to experience every bit of the small-town charm. She had found her home with Silas.

The showcase was much like a variety show and would be a wonderful attraction for guests at the new hotel. The winner of the three-legged race always determined where the showcase would be held.

"Just remember, we have to beat Weezer. She cheats and wins every year. But not this year. This year I will see to it that the showcase spot goes to the hotel." Silas beamed.

He had settled in nicely to life with modern conveniences, but he still needed space to be alone. She would give him whatever he wanted.

"How are you going to do that?" She had to admit that she was intrigued.

"I have a plan."

At the starting line, they tied a thick ribbon around their ankles. The sun was warm on her skin and the sky a bright blue, reminding her of Silas' eyes. Everything would remind her of him, and she wouldn't have it any other way.

Brad and Raf were also in the race, representing the orchard. She gave both men a wave and they hobbled over.

"We're winning this year," Silas said.

"So, we should just hang back then?" Raf looked between Silas and Brad.

"Make it look like you're trying. I don't want Weezer catching on." Silas loosened the ribbon around their legs.

"What are you doing?" she said.

"Don't worry. You'll know when it's time."

"Who is Weezer racing with?" Brad said, trying not to point.

Weezer River, apparently as much a fixture as Silas and someone he liked and admired, was in a class by herself. The devil by day and an angel at night when no one could notice. She wore her hair coiffed and sprayed into place. Claudia wasn't sure if running in combat boots was a good idea, but hey. To each his own.

"I don't know," Silas said.

"That's Corbin. Talbot's son. What's he doing here?" Talbot hadn't mentioned that Corbin was competing in the race. But it was nice to see him, standing tall and out of his military uniform. She could rest easier knowing he was safe on American soil for now. But she would still beat his butt in this race.

"Carter is the judge, and he's in on the plan. Sticks, when he says go, just run. I'll take care of the rest."

"I don't know how we're going to win. You're a foot taller than I am."

"Leave it to my dad." Brad pounded Silas' back and barked out a laugh.

"Runners, take your place," Carter said into a bullhorn.

They lined up. She didn't know the other competitors but there were quite a few, looking determined to win.

"I forgot to ask. How does Weezer cheat?"

"Go," Carter shouted.

Everyone took off. Silas held her around the shoulders and pulled her along. She gripped his waist with her arm, trying to stay upright. Uneven ground around the duck pond made running with three legs harder than it could be. Spectators shouted, but all she could think about was not falling down. Brad and Raf were behind them, telling them to keep going.

Most of the other teams fell apart early on, making it seem like she and Silas had a chance. The boutique hotel was going to be a great addition to the town, and she wanted everyone to love it for Silas' sake. Having the showcase there would give the town an excuse to spend time there.

Weezer and Corbin passed them, but Silas didn't seem worried. Claudia couldn't believe what played out in front of her, but Weezer tripped one of the other teams. They went rolling, and Weezer cackled. Corbin turned his gaze on her, but shrugged and kept going.

"They're getting ahead," she said and tried to keep up with Silas who had shifted into a new gear.

"Hang on, Sticks. Here's where it's about to get good." Silas yanked his leg away from hers. The ribbon fell off and blew away. With both legs under her full command, she almost tumbled onto her face. He scooped her up before she hit the ground and took off.

"Silas, what are you doing?" She held on to him as she bounced in his arms.

He flew past Weezer and Corbin, leaving them in his dust. Silas and she crossed the finish line, and he deposited her on her feet next to Carter.

"The winners are Silas and Claudia." Carter held their hands in the air. People clapped and cheered.

"No way, old man," Weezer said, pointing at Silas. "You cheated. You can't carry your short girlfriend over the finish line. Carter, tell them."

"Give it a rest, love of my life. You've been cheating for years. Time for you to get a dose of your own medicine and let someone else host that holiday showcase for a change." Carter pulled Weezer against him and kissed her firm on the lips.

She huffed, pushed him away, and marched in the direction of the vendors. Corbin chased after her.

"Don't worry about her," Carter said. "She'll get over it. Congratulations to you both. Looking forward to having that showcase any place but my winery." Carter shook hands and followed in Weezer's footsteps.

"Nice job, Dad." Brad and Raf joined them. "Weezer deserved to lose this year."

"I think everyone is in agreement," Raf said. "I'm going to head over to Ember's cookie tent. Anyone want to join?"

"I will. Talk to you both later," Brad said and walked away with Raf.

"Ice cream?" Silas held her waist.

"How would you feel if we got our ice cream to go and ate it back at the guesthouse?" She might have to stop calling it that. Maybe owner's house had a better ring.

"Are you tired of the small-town festivities already?" He kissed her behind her ear, lingering for a second and sending scrumptious chills over her body.

"Not a chance. I love this whole thing. But now that we won, I want you all to myself in our quiet little home without any clothes on so I can lick the ice cream off you."

"No clothes and ice cream. Sweet deal. How about we race over to the stand, and the winner gets to decide where the ice cream goes." He arched a brow.

She placed a kiss on his lips. He had made her the happiest woman in the world, giving her everything she didn't know she wanted.

She held his gaze, and her heart bloomed. "I love you, Silas."

"I love you, Sticks. Ready to race? On three."

"One… three." And they ran.

ALSO BY STACEY WILK

Serenity Series

Sea Glass Made with Second Chances

Sea Glass Hidden in Plain Sight

Sea Glass Out of Balance

Sea Glass Wrapped in Red

Heritage River Series

The Risk for House and Home

The Bridge Between Love and Lies

The Essence of Whiskey and Tea

Hometown Series

Taking Root

Raising Winter

Defining Chances

Beginning Over

Steeling Hearts

Whispering Christmas

Winter at the Shore Series

No More Darkness

Through the Darkness

Light Upon the Darkness

The Brotherhood Protectors World

Winter's Last Chance

The Last Betrayal

Her Last Word

The Last Days of Christmas

Seduced by Denial

Chill in the Air

Fighting for Tessa

Nash's Promise

Cruz's Watch

Harlan Unleashed

Big Sky Country Series

Time Won't Erase

Stay Awhile

Love Never Ends

Dare to Tell (coming soon)

READY FOR ANOTHER TRIP TO CANDLEWOOD FALLS?

Enjoy these exciting Summer 2023 Releases!

If you want to find out more about Talbot, Claudia's assistant, and whether or not Talbot stays in Candlewood Falls read *Kisses Sweeter than Wine* by USA Today best selling author Jen Talty

If you want to fall in love with Van Wilde, Claudia's handyman, read *Wilde and Dangerous* by K.M. Fawcett

ACKNOWLEDGMENTS

From the moment I met Silas, I knew he would have his own book some day. I have to thank my faithful readers for loving him as much as I do and allowing me to share his story with them.

As always, I must thank Jen and K.M. for taking this journey with me. Whenever I say *we should do* they are always willing to come along for the ride. This world would not be possible without them.

I also have to thank my dear friend and writing companion, Lisa A. Olech. If it wasn't for her expertise and calm demeanor, I would still be standing on the ledge of *Oh my God, my book just fell apart*, flapping my arms like a high-stressed humming bird.

I will always give the loudest shout out to my reader extraordinaire Robin. She is a big part of my process and I couldn't do this without her.

I probably should thank my family. Ha ha! They have to put up with me while I create. And I love them for accepting my prickliness during the tough parts.

I can never thank my readers enough. You make me an author. Without you, these are just black letters on cream colored pages, waiting to be brought to life by the imagination of the willing. Thank you for trusting me with your free time. I love you all.

～

ABOUT THE AUTHOR

From an early age, best selling and award winning author Stacey Wilk told tales as a way to escape. At six she wrote short stories in composition notebooks, at twelve she wrote a novel on a typewriter, in high school biology she wrote rock star romances in her binder instead of paying attention.

But it wasn't until many years later, inspired by her children and a looming birthday, that she finally took her story-telling seriously. And published her first novel in 2013. Since then, she's gone on to publish thirty-one more so women everywhere could fall in love and find an escape of their own.

She isn't done telling stories. Not by a long shot. If you want to read her best selling, emotional, and honest books about family, romance, and second chances, visit her at www.staceywilk.com